Sawney's
And The Woe Of Roanoke

Mat Horton

Part 1

Book 1
The Ballad of Agnes Bean

Book 2
The Chronicle of Thomas Hume

Book 3
A Ruined Hume and Bean

Part 2

Book 4
Dimmock's Yellow Diary

… So To Sawney Bean

Part 1

Book 1
The Ballad of Agnes Bean

23rd March 1603. Girvan, Scotland.

Narrator-
'Twas not just the gale that chilled his skin
As he mulled on the cannibal captured
within.
In trembling state he clenched his cane
To rap tap the gate of the jail in the rain.

Dour jailer bade enter, unbolted the door
And jolted the ragged convict on the floor.
He shook himself down to render some warm
Then span in alarm as she seized his arm.

Agnes-
"Close to me, notary!

Sit near if you dare…
Sunrise I'll swing from my tree of the hair.
Wring your wet cloak and I'll narrate
The tale of the thousand folks that was ate."

"Put quill to ink and I will tell
Of those that now burn in hell.
I'll tell of my past, that place I abhor
And them that scared Ayrshire
For years five and score."

"They say I'm a witch
Which I say to them nay!
I'm a Christian now,
I know how to pray.
I'm repented of sin, lamented the crime.
A new son's arrived. A husband who's kind.
And my slate to lave this last night I'm
confined.
But your words just might leave my men
unmolested
For I am the last of the Beans arrested…"

"He's your boy!"
"It's a brute"
"He's a Bean!"

"It's a mute"
"Och hold your son, Father, for he is no
freak"
"That it is blinkered wife,
 It's got whiskers and teeth!"
"He's smiling!"
"That's scowling. And why's it not howling?
I swear it by god it's laying there growling!
And hold it I'll not. In its pit eyes I've seen
That predators stare. I swear it's no Bean.
But a wolf clothed in a babes pink skin.
Imps have taken my innocent kin!
And swapped it with this…
A goblin twin!"

"He tore at the breast, saw jest in the wail
And so was suckled straight from a pail.
He came into the world callous and brawny
Alexander she named him.
They nicknamed him Sawney."

"He was kept in a pen most day and all night
'Cause for he could walk he would crawl for
a fight.
He bit all his brothers and strangled his pets
And snarled at his parents

And dismissed their threats."

"At night with the family fearful in bed
The yearling would laugh as he filled them
with dread.
He'd bark and howl as he smashed up his
room
And chillingly bout with himself in the
gloom."

"His Pa was crofting away in Killwinning
When Sawney, aged 7, wet his taste with a
killing.
He was grabbed in the fields by the twins
McTavish
Who trussed him in twin to beat him savage.

"You ugly Ned. Trespass you dare!
We'll bat your head and burn your hair
We'll break your arms, ten fingers and then
We'll beat you up for burning our den."

"The teens took turns to sear him with brands
From the fire he'd lit in McTavish's lands.
He roared through the pain, the smell and the
smoke

Then tolled their knell when he gnawed the rope."

"His Pa tried hard to teach him his trade
But Sawney the youth had only displayed
An utter contempt for manual work
And daily slunk off to rob from the kirk."

"An encounter at twelve whilst digging a ditch
Was a vicious tryst with a fiery bitch
Who smashed her fists into Sawney Bean
When taunted with smut
She deemed obscene"

'Fight like a man! You bit me! You swine!'

'Off me big wench. I'll snapeth your spine!'

"He tore at her clothes
She flattened his nose.
And gouged his eyes
And yanked his hair.
A counter attack laid bosoms bare.
Then bloodied and ripped he mounted the mare.

And then they were hitched.
Pa and the bitch.
She showed him tricks to make them rich.
She was his match in harsh and vice
And the pair of them both were the flip side
of nice."

"Before he had anger. With her came rage.
They planned to fly, escape the cage
Of laboring life in his ancestral home.
Fools had gold they'd claim their own."

"Flew the nest in early teens.
Trade was made by menacing means.
They found their way through the threat of a
flay.
Folks in fear for their lives would pay."

"Gert would flirt with drunks in the Inn.
Her trunked thighs seemed slim with gin.
She'd flounce them out with a kiss and a
grope.
Pa would pounce, his dirk to their throat."

'Now it's awakened! No. You'll not runaway.
Come to me lass for a roll in the hay.'

"By her hair he hauled her, this horny goat herder
Sawney in wait saw his third gory murder.
Now wanted for trial the pair of them fled.
Night times through towns hunting for bread
To the forest of Galloway, there to make camp
To give birth to the first in then cold and the damp."

"Address you your notes,
Nervous young clerk!
I was pressed out to the dark!
Five years in a pit with a fern for a door
A toil for food in the soil on the floor.
Rat and root and dreams of boar."

"Winter and wolves and snow on the ground
Saw sisters of mine buried under a mound.
Hunger pangs stabbed all us three.
Worse was the wail of the spirit banshee."

"Mother – curse her! Felt 'em inside her
When Pa, in the den, heard the sound of a rider.

Sprang out he with stealth and bought down
to the floor
A pitiful father of a family of four.

Not even a coin had the man when he died
By his groin dragged into our hide.
With famines thin fingers clawing within
He made us a meal from his first severed
limb."

"I sat and I watched and I ate and I learned.
By the glint in their eyes I saw that they'd
turned.
With blood spattered chins I saw it first then.
Addicts! That thirst for flesh of men!"

"The meat made Ma strong and after she bore
A triplet of boys. Then there came more.
Scores of poor riders died every year
'Till none ventured in to the forest of fear."

"Our home was a hall from the bones of the
mauled
With us now numbering ten.
Logan's laird for Reevers came
Through the woodland with all of his men."

"We scattered before the hand of the law
Rumbled our slaughter house midden.
Sawney I saw by Satan was driven
To the coast and a cavern near to Girvan."

"A serpentine tunnel, fathoms deep
Became his castle and our keep.
Out from this fume filled torchlit lair
He'd venture forth to plundered snare.
Those alone and sometimes pairs."

"From a child I grew and I witnessed lots
My toys were robbed off of eaten Scots.
My clothes the finest clothing stolen.
From wretched souls our bellies swollen."

"I alone he'd take to fairs
Our pockets wide with others wares.
There we'd stock with things we need.
He'd get blind drunk on honey mead,
Tell of his past and twisted creed."

"A starving start saw me late to bloom.
Fresh man flesh flowered five to groom.
He most needed mead supplies

And I could calm suspicious eyes."

"So I was special just to him
A small respite for it was grim.
An appetite unsatiated, eased a bit inebriated
Elspeth was the first pregnated.
Megan next then vexed Fannie
Dwarfish Elsie, cyclops Annie…"

"Half his army was his harem.
Hefty as the males and wild.
Bullied me to urchin minding,
I, the eldest, looked a child"

"Mother said-
'You'll ne'r produce!'
And started a chronic abuse."

"The Bean boys voices all got deep,
Bullocks bodies, minds of sheep.
With a band of bambinos to keep
Larger groups attacked and taken.
His cravings never seemed to slacken."

"In the cave I stayed! Kept far from danger.
I never went. Never killed a stranger!

Never allowed out on a raid
But stayed and worked a nursery maid.
Ma stayed too, a wet nursed turned
And I was beat and I was burned."

"But once a month and sometimes more
I'd leave the lair and there I saw
In Girvan town where folk where trading
Livings earned not got through raiding.
Good men, children, none deformed!
In secret thought 'I'll be reformed!
And do what's right and not grow old
A troglodyte! Doing what she's told."

"When the one eyed one birthed twenty two
Mother sat and refused to move.
Motionless in morbid rest,
Queues of bairns clamped her baggy breast.
For me she'd only rise, to batter.
The milkmaid sat and just got fatter."

"So many moons I tended brats and mended
wounds.
I skinned and dried the lifeless hides
And racked them in our store.
Mother did no chore because

She weighed the same as four."

"Able cadavers I would salt,
Boiling all those scrawny.
Stewed the parts to feed the clan
The heart was kept for Sawney."

"His idle state would slump away
When he ate that pump then he would bay
'I'll fight all eight!'
And then he'd wrestle
Massive sons gorged on gristle
And always win for Sawney Bean
Full of heart was thrice as mean!"

"Twas all the worse when the tide was high
Buried under ground. Away from the sky
Black and dank, with the mead drank dry.
Hiding blind amongst bairns for I had no bust
But I sensed his rage and I smelt his lust."

"We'd an unseen hole where the sea came to
swirl
Where none could fit but a waif.
In the dark echoed groans, screams and
moans

We shivered there wet but safe."

"When my chest at last did grow
I was whipped as father's beau.
The suckling sow sliced into me!
Cruel with insane jealousy!"

"You!
 With that nauseous look upon your face
For the things I tell of my disgrace!
I was raised a slave in a vampire's cave!
But I swear my souls been saved!
And I was but coal till he made me whole
So pen your scroll and don't shake with fright
For the things I tell on this stormy night
'Twas all before I saw Gods shining light."

"I'd never a friend save one carrion crow
Who came every day to be fed
Eye to eye it seemed to know
My depths of despair and dread."

"My abhorrent parent bent my mind!
I sought suicide and almost died.
I swam to the crag and nearly drowned,
Ran to the moor. I was always found

And then I was enraptured."

"In my dark despair shone a shaft of light
One autumn night, I was struck first sight
Then I cherished life when live Englishmen
were captured."

"Blue bloods, five, only half alive
And sixteen year old Timothy Demure.
Linked by chain and a world of pain
I cried in shame to think what he'd endure."

"They shuffled in, beaten men
And all had a dreadful pallor.
But by the wounds of the tribe
And Sawney's vibe
They must have fought with valour."

"His wrath was high for he'd lost an eye
And he grabbed me by my mane
'My tone is low so you will go
And bring me the heart of the Thane!"

"But the Thane he fought
When I sought his heart
For never a live one did.

And the triplets came to butcher the Thane
And Timothy I hid."

"Another night ambush he had planned
For in winter time was harder.
Ordered out his band under strict command
To stock high our sordid larder."

"Thus hid from the horde he spoke as a Lord
An accent I'd trouble translating.
But he made it clear, he was such a dear.
My fore fear was she who sat lactating."

"If father was a riot on his organ diet
Then brains as a mains the reverse.
None the sharpest flint.
Not one had a hint.
As food for thought they were worse."

"So he lay undiscovered
In the nest of the buzzard
My crush completely sealed.
And I tried not to show my innermost glow
Or reveal my angel concealed."

"The aristocrat hicks got eat in weeks.

When I felt his horror surge
I'd urge him peak by my nimble cheeks
Then I'd serenade him with a dirge."

"Neath a curtain of arms I ground my charms
Covert behind a wall of skulls.
When Tim would pall for an anguished bawl
I'd tell him the sounds were gulls."

"Till the shortest day I'd force a lay,
Pinned with a shackled leather tether.
Till the longest night and a promise of flight
When we'd both elope together."

"On the equinox morning I awoke with a
warning
That something was amiss.
Up slithered mother with a breakfast
undercover
And shattered my happiness bliss."

"Oh Agnes I've been wrong!
Eat this. Go on!
Better as a Mother I'll get!"

"A crocodile hug, offed the quadruped slug.

I broke the fast and then a sweat."

"With deep suspicion for her kindly mission,
A distrust of her most changed ilk.
I followed a smear as I'd lost my fear
Of a spiral of blood and milk."

"It bled to the head made fence.
I spied the open shackle, heard her broken cackle
My dire came back intense.
The hideous trail of the vast female
Thence went to her snug.
And smothered in a rug with her round face smug
Sat the leathered mound of she.
I uncovered the sheet.
There clamped to her teet
Was the head of Timothy."

"My grief was stunning. Tears were running
I snatched six foot of yew.
Dazed I raised the wood with which
I'd smash the fat bitch in two."

"Fazed for a second then Mother beckoned

With a laugh to lower the staff.
With my yearning burned
I froze when I turned…
For Sawney Bean had returned."

"The heart! His heart! She's ate your part!
She's drained your casks!
She claims divinity!
She's hid a lover undercover
And she's made her Mother suffer
The brunt so viscously!"

"For my life I did grovel
In the crab covered offal.
Crouched in painful cringe.
He raised his cane then thought again
For he'd got no Hogmanay binge."

"Heretic!
The clan were fuming. Throwing stones
And then exhuming Timmy's limbs
And throwing them. My face a bruise
And full of phlegm.
Death was looming, Sawney then
Bade them stop and hailed for silence
Stopped the stoning and the violence."

"Be still my flock! I've one last mission!
Before you rock it to perdition.
I'll make you come, blasphemous runt
To booze to buy and be my front!"

"Riding beside him, my neck in his claw
Sheer terror was striking but all the folk saw.
Was a Dad loading festive fare for a caper.
My mouth said nought but my eyes cried -
'Murder!!'"

"Cuffed to the cart from Girvan town
A dagger wrapped inside my gown
While Sawney whistled tunes at leisure
Contented with fermented pleasure.
For he had siphoned off a barrel.
My whole rang with predicted peril."

"With glassy eye the nasty lech
Eased his paw from off my neck."

"A favour! Then I'll set you free.
Sit! Teasing whore, upon my knee."

"By the fire in his eye

And his quick rank breath
I saw the lie. Saw rape saw death.
Sawney saw his double vim.
My heart and the heart of Tim."

"He plied himself, decanting liquor
Untied my bond, his panting quicker.
He reached out for my hair to stroke
I skewered his hand into the oak!
And jumped and ran the speed of wind
And yet he pumped, to drink was pinned."

"Camouflaged in a meadow
I heard him bellow, till the morrow
Then spur his ass.
But on I lay through night and day
Till my bones were froze in the grass."

"In the field I was found
By ploughman Brown
And the simpleton I've since wed.
I've been a good wife.
This sons my life!
But a tear for Tim is still shed!
Ten years past my past hit hard
So I went and found a savior.

I sought retribution and was given absolution
By a priest, for a sexual favour."

Book 2
The Chronicle of Thomas Hume

Narrator-
The solemn scribe, sore Thomas Hume
Stood slow and strode the room.
A thunderous crack didn't change his tack
And his face was a mask of doom.

Thomas-
"Ten whole years! Five hundred men!
That dismal decade should've ended then!
Think of all those lives not saved
When you were Not the vampire's slave!"

"Innocent play upon the shore
With friends abound and then no more.
Because of grizzled finds of gore.
Then my boyhood shriveled and ceased
When I was shielded from the beast."

"In solitary isolation.
No playmate to grace my station.
A little hell, hotel Stranraer!
Sick at night from all the fear!
Stiff with fright for year 'pon year.
What other suffers might it bring?
This spectral wicked winged thing."

"But what was worse was my seclusion,
Worse than all demon delusion.
Lonely. Only hotel guests
Would spare a word before their quests.
It came to this - I'd face the fate!
If I could just play with a mate."

"One nightmare night when I fourteen
I woke to find a nightmare scene.
The sky was bright from flame of torch
And piercing it was spear and fork."

"The sheriff with a punk band baying
Accused my father of the slaying.
Told him of the evidence.
Then built a gallows from our fence."

"We had board six English types.
One a Lord and four were Knights.
And the dandies from the south
Had signed the hotel log book out."

"I screamed to Jesus 'Pray it stop!'
-The hangman was a man of frock.
The noose was tightened by the parson.
A forced recluse, now half an orphan."

"I held his feet so he could save
A final word before his grave…

'Thomas Hume, I've groomed thee strong
So go my son and right the wrong.
Seek you the truth and with the proof
Proclaim our name with pride again."

"So I'm not scared!
And my nerves are not frayed!
The emotion is hate! That's been displayed
And I'll pity you not, foul Agnes the black
For you could have told to turn the tide
back."

"Ostracized! And while we mourned

Panes were broke and paint adorned .
Mother scorned, as other owners
Of taverns who had hosted rovers.
The landlord of the inn at Ayr
Hung as hikers last seen there.
The publican of the pub 'The Bear'
Lynched by just a signature."

"And many more, their loved ones too
Grieving when the mob charged through.
Any hamlet near and where
Bones were washed up from the mer."

"A reject in her own commune
Mother saw no oppurtune.
A lunacy saw naked stray
She off the cliff at Moroch bay."

"Necessity uplifted me!
I sold the abode and I hitched on carts
To Edinburgh and education.
I wrote reports on the renegade courts
And of the missing gripping the nation."

"My psyche was scarred. Street life was hard
So I turned a bard for my bread.

Reams I filled with the streams of killed.
I wrote in a broad sheet spread"

"I wrote in verse for prose was worse,
The crimes in rhymes were shorter.
The Edinburgh Times bought up my work
Then employed me a court reporter."

"My odes on the rogues soon ran to the road
Of regal recognition.
All the travesty inked I was goad to be linked
To his majesty and audition."

"I entered his chamber the wordsmith painter.
A favoured Makar macabre.
In his innermost ring I had swung the swing
To a patronage from a pauper."

"I feigned effete for the Royal seat
To list all lives been lifted.
Although my work now obsolete
I penned the deceit of the twisted."

"Heed priests whore! Desist your wail!
Shut up your awful yelling!
It is almost dawn and as last of the spawn

You'll listen, for there's more needs telling.
'Tis of your kin that I'm steeped in sin,
I played the gay laureate
'Twas pride for my name
That I suffered the shame
And rode the Kings wicked chariot!"

"So in Scotland's west still more arrests
In the hamlets, towns and shanties.
And the people fled or stayed in dread
Of the ghoul or the vigilantes."

"Tracks went sparse from mass clearance
In reaction to the slaughter.
And on it went, the disappearance
With scores rent off every quarter."

"And all the prayers in all the Kirks
And all the pens from all the clerks
Writing up such vast rewards
And fighting men with sharpened swords
In mustered crews, try they might
Could not flush the phantom blight."

"A chain of plays I thus obtained
From the tide of pain in the tyrants reign.

'Till a fortune shift in a winters mist.
Love slain in fey terrain."

'Stop calling me Belle!' Pleaded Claire
She said as she sat on her colt from the fair

'Please stop, else after we're wed
That silly name I'll be known instead'
Said Captain Enn of the foot regiment
'Your beauty it doth make my heart
resonant.'
She reached to touch him
'Ride close to me'
As a cloaking fog rolled from the sea."

"Out from the silent smokey white
A violent croak that put to flight
Her mount. And then a pack of beasts
Materialized with screams

'BEAN FEASTS!"

"A horde of forty freaks came roaring
Swarmed then struck and then got goring
The horse that had sat Claire astride
And killed the Colt and the would be bride."

"Enn fought on as on they flooded.
Witnessed his betrothed get gutted.
Slashed his blade, banged both his gun.
A sound of a drum and the scum were gone."

"Merchants in numbers, crossing the night
Spotted the officer in his fight
And rode to his aid to join the affray
The savages then simply melted away."

"Proof! With Enn and his lost bride
That the scourge of the land was but a tribe.
A monstrous tribe of killers, skilled
But brutes who bled and could be killed!"

"The captain rode to Holyrood.
Inside the palace in somber mood
Sought an audience with the King
And told him of the odious sting."

"The King was throned with Anne the Dane
And he well knew of witches bane
For limping to the Firth of Forth
'The Gideon' hit from a storm boiled north."

"His childish bride implied black magic.
Swore she spied a cursed pelagic.
Back in Denmark repercussions
Found a slew of Satan's covens."

"Scotland also women burned.
The massed trials was where he'd learned
Of sorcery, his expertise
To write 'The Demonologies."

"The Samson hag had howled a scorcher.
Confessed a verse whilst under torture,
That Satan's foe upon this earth
Was James 6th and soon the 1st."

"And so the King his ear was keen
To hear of tell of Sawney Bean.
Requested his Castalien band

'Compose me ditties of the damned."

"Cast as hero in the title,
Routing evil by the bible.
A fictitious righteous homicidal
He checked the text for signs of libel."

"My story stirred him up a storm
To arm his army in the morn.
Commanded Enn to navigate
To where he'd come eradicate."

"His Highness led the holy force
Four hundred men and forty horse.
Sniffer dogs to sniff the rot,
Four cannon and some cannon shot
And gunpowder to blow their plot."

"A friend's was Enn as we trekked the glen
Solace in our loss.
But we were not wiser men
As we thought they troops of moss."

"Some sung songs stomping the prairie
To calm the King when he got wary
Harassed from a past kidnap
He asked his cortège-
'Falter back"

"The coast was hunt to Bannane head
Till dusk had set without a thread.
Then a musky scent of dead

Was scented by a sniffer hound.
The fiendish cave was finally found."

"Six abreast with fixed bayonets
We marched into a mire.
Shadow things gleamed harrowed scenes
Born of brandished fire."

"Nerves were spent as dreams were bent
In purple circled gaze
Flambeaux sticks played demon tricks
On the walls of the garbled maze."

"James who was by far a fool
Halted by a sunken pool
And thus defended by the fosse
Said –
 'Strum minstrels! Before the cross."

"And as they stayed and played and prayed
I, Enn and skittish men
Marched to fetid maw.
A crab brigade held us at bay
For they had raised claw."

"To reeking ink we flinching inched

When a rat gang scampered, rabid.
Shooted caps swarmed storms of bats
And warned that we'd invaded."

"The stifled quiet after rifles fired
Cracked the cavity.
Then eyes got burned as we turned and
learned
Of wracked depravity."

"We bumped about in sickened blunder,
Sick in mind and drenched in chunder.
Our souls were so torn asunder
In the charnel pit of people plunder."

"Seven stacks of salted corpses!
Baskets of torsos, main courses.
Soup tureens of human beings
Nibbled ears in pickle jars
Eyeballs in an ornate vase.
A store of sawn off gnawed on arses!"

"Seared in morbid awe we stood
A soldier leaked a lake of blood
Panic stricken torches fell
Then another's fatal yell."

"Rushed on the Goth! With a rage of wroth
And chaos cleaved the ranks
A hatchet heaving crazed behemoth
Hewed a swathe in our flanks."

"She led a hate filled hurricane
A heinous typhoon.
It slammed into our barricades
And ploughed through the platoon."

"Nine men died. Four more would die
More knelt for mercy's pity
Thence came a clear rung battle cry
Which shored us all with gritty"

"Pro Rege Et Lege!
Defend the liege!'
Aroused the rousing shout.
The captain broke the siege to bend
The battle from a rout."

"Kindled privates raised to rally
Muskets spat a leaden volley.
Vengeful swords pricked many more.
Enn ripped on –

'The King! The law!'
Till all that was defiant
The mammoth axe wield matriarch
And her mirrored triad giant."

"Sacrilege! None shall pass!
Defile his snooze-ed church!'

The mothers trine lurched to sign
A necro oozing mass."

"Hails of slugs drilled four fat thugs
But on they fought on, praying.
Swung sword and axe till shells collapsed
Emptied with the spraying."

"Gunpowder booms saw sulphur fumes
Form layered waves of brume.
A shadow loomed in hazed gloom
Smoked out his basest tomb."

"The grog soaked ogre, half hungover
Eyed his empires fall.
Dead or caught the air was fraught
As he prowled with a dual maul."

"But ire was in the eye of Enn.
His spouse assassin now he ken!
His passion grew to fired glow
He steeled to pounce.
To smite his foe."

"Sawney's daunting presence failed.
Crumbled, paled. He tumbled, nailed.
His glowered glare blurred to stoned.
The bully beat. Chained and owned."

"Unclean fiend!
James preened behind a wall of armed ward.
His clique of poets notebooks primed
For histories record.

"Force it kneel. May fierce it feel
The justice of our Lord!
Your souls to pay on judgement day.
Today you'll bless your King.
You'll beg me grace for this disgrace
So yield! And kiss my ring!"

"The ogre bridled. Dangled guards.
Strode towards, spoke with barbs.
Fettered, held and half blind drunk

Still scared the King and sucked his spunk."

"Kneeling? Yielding? Kissing rings?
No more talk of witless things!
For we both Kings and sires of mice
And are we not both mired in vice?"

"I reap souls and rape a few.
Are souls also thy own taboo?
I seen so, seen your mincing crew!
There is a difference twixt us two…
Your fret of me! Not I of you!"

"Twas at that moment from the pool
Infants from a horror school
Clamped his padded pants like leeches.
The King released and soiled his breeches."

"He screamed a stream of cussing words,
The likes of which I'd never heard

"A cussed towel!"

"His bowel the lighter.
More an author than a fighter."

"As biting brats were beaten back
The Kings façade began to crack.
What before a cod piece itch
Exploded as a nervous glitch."

"He dropped his rood to rabbit bounce
Howled in bandy legged flounce.
Howls of haunts of headless mums
And cussed repents of sodding sons."

"Sawney and his hellish brood
Smirked in relish at the lewd
Eccentric monarch on display.
James, ashamed, vowed they would pay."

"Forty seven cannibals
lugged out to mornings light
They mocked him locked in manacles,
Jeered on in wounded plight."

"Jeering all the march duration
Acting the Kings defamation
 Ornery taunting flaunting bilboes
In the swamps betwixt the enclose
Of Tollbooth's incarceration
James citing rightful divination

And to avoid his abdication
Ordered a mass mutilation."

"From the raucous throng were ripped
Their glottis tongues and dogs were tipped.
A slippy slope thence I slipped."

"The family thrown in an oubliette.
My stance seen as a sovereign threat.
My expulsion from the August members.
A week which saw my words as embers."

"Censors raided publish places
Papers pulped or burnt to ashes
Cinders made of any cases
Of literature containing traces.
Any hint of this affair
Written or whispered would ensnare."

"Back on the street out the Jacobean elite
Poor pay packets pending.
He pledged my course -
'The tower or worse!
 If you write again offending!"

"The Judge was Gruesome.

The charge high treason.
No defense. Not a voice could reason.
Yanked by ox to Leith's port market.
The men folk chained to form an orbit."

"The women watched atop their pyres
As Bean stalks wrenched off with pliers.
They added to the mound of meat
With severed hands and severed feet."

"Sawney was the last expire.
Stomped bloodied stumps
In a tongueless blare.
They waited till his ire got quenched.
Then they fired three pyres
Of his weans and wenches."

"The screams of weans bore a burden hard.
Worse was the sound as my books were
charred.
The cheers of the crowd soon tired and died
As the fire bit weans were the last Beans
fried."

"Silence settled on the square.
Their ashes sailed to snow the air.

A lone crow stared his murderous stare.
Then a warning to attending there
From Crown control a proclamation –

"To tattlers – trial and convication!
To any who speak of this they'd seen.
To the tattered quiet compensation.
Those at a loss 'cause of Sawney Bean."

Book 3
A Ruined Hume and Bean

24th March 1603

Thomas-
"So I stand pinched but yet can clinch
A trump of a scoop to gloat
For your priest revealed
That the son that you shield
Is His! - Which he sold for a groat."

"A crazed male cattle gored your old man's tackle,

His Bulls did'nae spore his wife.
I've a tale to grip the rabble
It'll claw back my flawed life"

"A best seller read! Half demon brood
And half the seed of the cloth!
Your son is star in my book bizarre
Saga of the church and the goth."

"And I want you know as its time to go
Bend the bows of your tree
That every Bean sowed and the bane that
they bowed
Will end with this story!"

Agnes-
"I was a slave in a vampires cave!
I'm a victim, as is thee.
If you've a heart you'll not impart
My boys identity.
Tear up your text and spare his neck
Print you'll snare an innocent!
End your revenge insistence!
Persevere and this I'll swear
I'll hex your short existence!"

Narrator-
It took two guards to tie her arms
Another to smother her voice
Took another two to secure the lasso
Together they heaved the hoist.

Creaked the branch that hung the minx
That clawed the hemp for air.
Not one dared glimpse her bulged glare
For fear fall foul of her jinx.

Agnes-
"No! 'Tis wrong. He's my golden one!
Let his future flourish.
A living hell will follow on,
I'll bet, if he's to perish!"

Narrator-
She tried to twist to lock the look
To deal the debt of Thomas.
To her choked despair he offed his stare
Her threat became a promise."

Agnes-
"Spirit of scourge! I command
A summons please of thee!

With thy black hand disease the land
In his vicinity!"

Narrator-
The stoked curse invoked a storm,
A deluge on the downcast morn.
Rain clouds were darkened further more
By crows with 'Murder!' in their caw.

She wailed in sway till she went grey
Limp fell her tiny fists.
The town folk say that to this day
Her grieving ghost persists.

As Agnes' demise pronounced
A courier cantered in, announced
'Bess is dead! Long live the queen!'
And folk forgot the hanging Bean.

The menace loomed as was presumed
From the Stuart regime
Soon Alba swept for secrets kept,
To keep his image clean.

A hasty London migrate
The theatre thrill an aim.

Disguised he merged with compromised
Falsified new name.

Thus part crusade of the puppet parade
Who came to curry favour
In Southwark's sinful suburb stayed
To soak the stimulus flavour.

Some happy weeks in cloistered streets
He sauntered to inspire.
Too distract to ink of the vibe and the stink
He planned a moons retire.

A month's long hibernation
With supplies to feed his need.
Sat scribbling expositions
For thespians to read.

Huddled in a hovel on the saga that he
planned
Thomas at his novel noticed not the noxious
land.
Alighted at his writing desk he'd only quit to
sleep
Did not notice pestilence had galloped in to
reap.

The manuscript completed he emerged to
copper sun
Then dropped the print in shock and squint
Saw what had thus become.
He strayed dismayed to theatre town
The start his souls decay-
The playhouses were closed down…
The plague had come to play.

In squat distraught by the padlocked wrought
Iron gates of 'The Globe'
Reflecting at his luckless lot
His conscience self in probe.

And as he analyzing
For answers for this state
A threat bade up him rising
Up face to face his fate.

"A boy to rent? A city gent?
Lodging in my manor!"
A cutlass pressed to ego dent
By the muggers manner.

Arrested in penury, pondering this strife

Up surged a misted fury
Which flipped the threatened knife.
When the mist had melted and tempest had
becalmed
An anxious ringing riled him
As regard the vagabond.

The sound was but tinnitus stress
Assumed a watch mans whistle.
He braced escape the stepped recess
And perforated gristle.

He paused to pluck the robbers purse,
The white noise was decreased
So stopped surveyed Agnes' curse
Saw what she had released…

This pulsing place that now was raw
A crucifix on every door
The grass that grew where trundled carts
As merchants moved to further parts.
No artistes left to grace the arts
Save painters with a raft of red
To cross the spot where dwelled the dead.

The damaged pimps with famished whores

As punters sniffed the bubo sores.
Unmanaged pits with silent cheers
Mere memories of the bitten bears
And fighting cocks with un-bet claws.

Prophetically, a leak of laughter
The promised pox had carved disaster.
Swept through sewers, cellars, rafters
It squeezed the dogs and sneezed the masters
Panicked the preachings of the pastors.

Oily rats as slick as foxes
Breakfasted in rancid boxes
Boxes full of blackened corpses
Stacked by those whose hacking coughing
Would soon fill a stacking coffin.

This hub of industry derailed
As ailing London's heartbeat failed.
Still the city stink prevailed…

In desolate delirium he reeled in disbelief
Then sought a whore emporium to dicker
some relief.

"Pray enter!" Bade the brothels Ma'am

"Drink to our decline!"
For the prostitutes had looted
A polluted shop of wine.

Pickled in a drunken trance
To part forget, to part enhance
The tickled perfumed tender first
Female touch that purged his purse.

He swigged in swing his quart of ale
Spurting to her fickle wail
Bangs not heard as spurt on time
The hammered nails of quarantine.

Shut up in dark without a meal
Fumbling, finding things by feel
Feeling kegs but needing bread
Felt the rigor mortis dead.

Caged in the contaminated boudoir!
Crazed in a claustrophobic stupor
As fevered tarts with oozing marks
Farted as he starved.

He drank to numb what he'd become.
His buggered life in tatters.

Muggers blood in sleep he swum
Of which he still bespattered.

One by one in shuttered gloom
The dying doxies raved their doom.
One by one the pleasure rooms
Came to be contagious tombs.

His rasping harlots final rantings
Played imaginations feared.
With this last call girl departing
Horrific mirages appeared.

His stomach stewed in bile and beer
In addled altered stance,
Famine straddled him to jeer
Joined Mort and Pestilence.

Three awful figures in cavort
Ruminated an abort,
To yearn the germ to end his life
For he had not crutch of child or wife.
And he had no pride just waves of shame.
Hunger plundered him insane.

Cradling his fading maid

In faint hallucination
Saw the brothel Sawney's cave
With Sawney in ovation.

A salivating fantasy
Thoughts he fought to plug
Sawney hailed him family
Applauded bloody stub.

Kaleidoscopes of woe and hope,
Groped knockers, black in taint.
A mocking demon tempted tope
'Abstain!'
Yelled shoulder Saint."

Refreshed!
With budding breast of Jezebel
And emptied jugs of ale
He feasted on infected Belle
Where ecstasy prevailed.

Sated with the tepid tit
He closed red eyes of rheum
Then froze he stiff in terror fit
As Sawney filled the room.

"Bore more, my heir. To reap your prize!
This feasts initiation.
Take heart, arise! For I will share
My kingdom of damnation!"

And it was odd to hear this laud
As tongueless his dictation.

Then his hanging father, with opposing slant
Harangued him hanging opposite
A rope rasping the rant

"Adopted by the cannibal?
A savage sod I've groomed!
Your foster father forced thy
Soul forever doomed.
For Eve you've eat urgo upset
Omniscient God!"

Giant triplets maneuvered
Embraced their sibling quad.

Powerless in sodden sheets
To shake the freakish dream
Gertrude Bean held piquant teats
And filled his mouth with cream.

Gagging on the pungent milk
A further fail to waken bilk
With carrion mother showering guilt
Harrying with –
"It's all your fault!"

In his hazed dreamscape jungle
Her assault saw Thomas crumble.
The baked Bean bairns hoorayed their uncle.

Victims that he never knew
Lined up torment him in a queue.
Stiff soldiers sang in symphony
Conducted by sir Timothy.

The philharmonic force of eaten
Sought to be some sort of beacon
To sway step sisters incest lusts,
Thrusting lice infested tufts.

Two armies faced each other
On psychotic plains.
An eroticizing coma
As the virus coursed his veins.

A horny flame haired Sawney
And the Devils feral pack
Fought fantastic in their fury
In the fray as prey fought back.

The quarry in the orgy
As decayed as zombie fiend
Sang frisky songs of glory
Of revenge on Sawney Bean.

Four horsemen of apocalypse
All gathered now and three
Galloped round the battlefield
Round War, the referee.

Twelve nights were like twelve lifetimes
With every second Hell.
Two weeks, too weak to turn his cheek
To block his beak the smell.

A fighting, biting, fornicating
Fortnight 'midst the mass.
Bubonic brass the audience
In scenes see Bosch aghast.

Paralyzed in excrement,

But that what shat him most…

Malevolence personified
In Her passion powered ghost.

Searchers scouring back end alleys
Tasked to find blighted bodies.
The bagnio reached to sanitize
When they heard inside his haunted cries.

Tearing boards of the bordello doors
They found him fitting on the floor.
He bit the grabbing hands of creatures.
The searchers had Agnes' features.

Bound atop the body truck
His clouting arms tight tied
Gagged with rags of bedding, dragged
To an Alms house. Dumped outside.

Spanning all of Autumn,
He raved the winters husk.
His burden London Sodom
He disbousomed dawn till dusk.

And no escape in slumber

When return to Sawney's cave.
An involuntary spelunker
In the bunkers of his brain.

"It's all your fault!'
The sick all cried
'It's all his fault!'
Before they died.
Grim miasma's of discord
As the reaper scythed an empty ward.

They tried in vain assuage his pain
But was a thankless task
For what he saw the nurses wore
A cursing Agnes mask.

And when they tried to soothe with words
Spoken soft in poise
All he ever heard was a
Spiteful poisoned noise.

And when they tried massage his skin
Silk fingers stroked his limbs.
All he ever felt was ten
Scratching steel pins.

Till winters thaw a laboured chore
His mentality infernal.
The malady rid 'twas their main bid
The infirmary back to normal.

Spring released the nurses ceased
Indulge his lunacy
His nightshirt seized and six girls heaved
Him out to a jubilee.

There the gentle poet
Who'd been pushed to a pariah
Partook with passing plethora
Who were praising a messiah
What he thought London's morph
Into Gomorrah
Turned to be a polished place
With a gala aura.

With flowers strung above the mews
And flags. And food on barbecues.
The crowds enthusing on the march,
Pressed sips of wine to lips of parch
They swept him to a towered arch.

Addled for an actor in antique attire

Up he raised onto the dais
With toga togged choir.
Seldom felt him welcome
So his spirits soared
As the Roman actors welcomed him aboard.

The reverberating rostrum was in bosting
beat.
Thomas full of frolic now in design to greet
The object of their ardor
Perhap' replenish emptied zeal
The performers splayed in grovel,
Horizontal, to reveal
A perfect panorama
With the plebeians prostrate.
The procession was a picture
Progressing to the gate.

But noticing their focus and he shattered like
a glass,
Unleashing floods of venom
At the sight of such a farce.

A pretentious farce as plastic
As this plaster arch constructed
For he that so corrupted

That he persecuted persons
Having parallel persuasions.

He! Producer of that righteous read
That castigating bigots creed.
Authorizing executions
Of Samuels semblancing Susan's
Whilst practicing the very acts
To contradict his gospel 'facts'.

For hailing in a fancy carriage
Hamming. Fronting a sham marriage.
He who aved the peasantry
As if from Caesars pedigree
Was James the poof who sat aloof
With offspring ringed
To guise his gayness
To resemble two faced Janus.

The play was all a fallacy
For this fraud and Pharisee.

The charade that passed the podium
Was stared in utter odium.
In disgust that flushed his looks
At the burner of his books

At the censor of his words
At the fawn of moron herds
Fallen posing in revere
Brown nosing for the premier
This premier with prim veneer
Who'd fucked him,
Then fucked his career.
Slew all but silent sycophants.
A psycho since he shat his pants.

He erupted off the pulpit
To the car, to scar the culprit.

The slobbering monarch wept in horror
Seeping piss and voiding honour
Pegged his possessed paramour,
Petrified at what he saw.

His ex-pet swearing vendetta
Roaring 'Rape!'
To souse him wetter.
Citing crimes of blood James spilled
Of the witness flood he'd killed.
For the shower of lovers spurned
For the cowering women burned.
For the poets pride forsaken.

For his art and arse he'd taken.

James to save his oily skin
Hid beneath his infant kin.
He shielded under Charles his son
As it shouted 'Charlatan!'

Forward fanned four Agnes clones
Who floored the tramp
And broke his bones.
On the orders of Lord Enn
Who saw him not, a former friend
But his onus eyesores cleanse
So threw the anus in the Thames.

Inhaling lungs of sucking slime
Was much a blessed release
For with the pain the poltergeists
Appearances had ceased.

Even comprehending that his bane
Was James the Queen
His mark of expiration was
The hark of Agnes Bean.

Part 2

Book 4

Dimmock's Yellow Diary

16 years previously.
Spring 1587. London, England.

Humfrey Dimmock-
'Twas almost May, the weather gay,
In London on 'The Lion'
Cowards some. Some slipped away,
In slipped the Devils scion.

One twenty tonnes with twenty guns
Raised by Raleigh's purse.
Sails unfurled to the new world.
'The Lion' shipped the curse.

The settlers cheered, 'The Lion' veered
Old Thames' estuary

They'd left their lives to sink or strive
A distant colony.
Sink or strive. Die or survive
We headed out to sea.

We aimed toward America
A strange land I didn't know
They prayed, the companies clerica
But still a storm did blow.

The boat it rocked- lunged left to right
Just later in that week
We had not passed the Isle of Wight,
I lost my joyous streak.

A hurricane to drain my vim.
We bounced like barreled balls.
None could hold their stomachs in
In spiteful Satan squalls.

Spit and spew sloshed the decks
As doubt drenched every mind
White spake-
 'What Warlock placed this hex?'
As England left behind.

The Devils spawn spurned on the storm
Like acid in a potion.
We were flimsy fodder for
The fuming spume shot ocean.

Euphoria was emptied.
With nerves set all a quiver
We a minute matchstick on
An endless friendless river.

I seasick and I homesick,
A fortnight from our shores.
The sweaty ship it stink of shit
When passed those green Azores.

In amidst of thumping thunder
Off strayed our sister sloop
But the pilot yearned for plunder
Refusing to regroup.

He ignored the Governor's orders,
Belittled Whites displeasure.
His sailors pirate hoarders
Of plundered Spanish treasure.

The flyboat lost, we shook, we tossed,

Dry peas waxed in a rattle.
And still he'd root about for loot
And treated us like cattle.

I vocalized the verdant lies
Of Raleigh's promised paradise.
Salt spray stung my scoured eyes,
I gormandized by parasites.

The lice, the lies, the nauseous sap,
I hankered tack for home.
I hankered back, reverse the map
Reverse this reckless roam.

When it becalmed the boredom bit,
In doldrums on the brine
The buccaneering foreign git
Was nicknamed now 'the swine.'

As tedium set I soon beget
To find out things to know.
'Twixt the pilot and the scion
I wished a storm to blow.

I wished a wind to wash them off
But 'twas a balmy breeze.

I wished it wild take off the child,
Wash off the Portuguese.
I wished a gale to break the jail
To free me on the seas.

As if in jail, the ambience
Was like a steaming kettle
'Twas the buck that pushed his luck
To try to test the mettle
Of swabs against the settlers.
Slurred those who'd set to settle.

He'd whisper lies, antagonize
Both sides, from stern to bow
He'd fucking thrive on raucous tides
And relish every row.

Fights with fists and arguments,
Pioneers, marines.
The men incensed, in their defense
'Twas smears and smoke screens.

Sussed by the assistant Howe
Who sussed the source of strife
Howe banished him remain below
For slandering the wives.

They put him down, that blue Bill Brown
To bunk amongst the men
To help the cook, by brutish look
Still swear he less than ten.

Less than ten down from the Glen
A Scot in tongue and hair.
Swamp green eyes held hate and lies
Stilled fear with sullen stare.

That stare glared out that turquoise mask
Spelt of hysteric wroth
Of that Scot would take to task
All that crossed his path.

The cook, a brigand, Johnnie Bright
Known for thuggery
Had lost, lay low, was fret to fight
Bill in the scullery.

For weeks he'd piss into the dish,
Slops had rat bones found
He'd grin and spit and say it fish
That beast, the Blue Bill Brown
Then raise his fists and all would wish

He buried in the ground.

And it was only Governor White
A good man, friend and boss
Insisted on his life's respite
Stopped to the deep sea toss.

It was the Governors luckless word
That staid their hands to kill
They should've flipped him overboard
To save them all from Bill.

They could have lived in calm accord
And all be thriving still.
If they'd have thrown him overboard
And saved themselves from Bill.

Puritan prudes still heard the lewd
Accounts of acts obscene.
Said stories rude to stoke the feud
'Twixt husbands and marines.

Scandal! The damage dealt.
The tension trailing he.
Howe and help both whipped a welt
Right to the Carribbea'.

Beard whipped a welt in Blue Bills pelt,
We blind to escapees.

Two Irish ran. They saw the signs
When dropped at last our anchor.
The bailing slime were papist swines
That added to our rancor.

It came to light that both they might
Both Catholic and bigot.
Both had rode before with White
Could guide a Spanish frigate.

With fearful thought of being caught
Or of a mutiny
Fernandez fraught and so he sought
To keep us out at sea.

But land! Oh blessed be the Lord!
Like rats we ran and then we poured
The sand to scrub the months of grime
And for a time our spirits soured
To feel our feet upon the ground.
Warm beer was cheered and passed around.

I sat upon sweet terra firma

Whilst scented breezes softly murmured.
For there a time the pining's yield
To see again an English field
And smell again a summer meadow
Or hark again a homily echo.
To fear not a fraught tomorrow.

So sat we under balmy palms
To sun ourselves and be becalmed.
A pilgrim preached a placid psalm...

Twas not long fore things went wrong
Again by witchery
Gathered fruit seared every throat,
Scorched hot in misery.

What island Sprite had we upset?
Were it the hold held ghoul?
Unslaked our burning throats with wet
Fire from a pool.

Flaming throats from poisoned ponds
Threats from those who chose abscond
An unsticking of our glue
From the hostile harried crew.
Sickness on the ship of woe

We sailed again to slick unknown.

Those taut weeks the tempers frayed.
To the Spics the boat betrayed
Arms were readied for a raid.
The greedy pilot sought to stray
From our pre planned destinations
To rob the gold off Spanish galleons.

The swine's sole goal was for a groat
His itch outshone the mission
From dawn to dusk he tore the throat
Of White's triumphant vision.

They cussed it was each other's fault.
Swine would not stop the ship for salt.
Waves of cloying awesome hot
Saw stinking food to start to rot.

Rot set in the crew aboard,
Fernandez formed the foe.
I faced the foe that chased the hoard
Than face the thing below.

The thing below was maddened now,
His lunacy was ripe.

He rippled in his hate for Howe
Whipped to a wicked gripe.

And on and on and on our way
In undulating sheets of grey
Slumped and sour and getting sicker
Sick of the constant grinding bicker.

Hot sun blazed braw upon burnt necks
Beat us down to sprawl scorched decks
I fade - but faced his foreign fire
Than shade to face that orphans ire.

So slumped and sick and hot and hungry
I riddled through with doleful doubt
In wane, the furnace fogged me dumbly
To not defy the profane lout.

And then a shout of 'Land Ahoy!
Oh how we thumped our backs with joy.
All old rifts were healing over
We cheered as if the cliffs of Dover.

It was a good and godly sight
The first my glimpse upon the might-y
'Merica, our task to master.

The pastors prayed us from disaster.

My heart in flutter with the honour.
Proud to represent the Crown.
A rush to rowboats on thrown ropes,
The sailors helped to swing us down.

We rowed onto the Roanoke
We blessed. We chosen few
Exalt as every oar stroke
Propelled toward our noble coup.

Twas faraway from Chesapeake Bay
But ranked our happiest times
We beached the craft then walked our way
Through many of mystique pines.

The scent of pines, exciting times
We stumbled on the fort…
Nought but that that spoke such crimes
That caused this posts abort.

Dwellings down, vacated,
Cinders signaled torching.
I felt a wraiths stirred hatred
That spelt an omen warning.

Where were the men of earlier?
Where Francis Drake's slaves?
The mystery far murkier
Than those encircled waves.

We whittled all the woods around
For signs of Grenville's men
But little there and little found
And little did we ken.

Little did we ken but we
Safe and sound ashore
We'd conquered the Atlantic sea,
Which filled with dogged valour.

We'd conquered and we'd bought the Lord
To where the Lord was not
We claimed it by his righteous sword
And hallowed first this plot.

A vote was cast, we'd stay a while
Convert this spot to Zion
We'd stay upon this arcane isle
And scorn the stinking 'Lion'.

'The Lion' that felt like the pit
Tight tempers running raw.
A bastard piloting the ship,
A fiend locked in the store.

But here we were as men reborn
In lands that we felt free
Trees were felled and logs were sawn
In England's colony.
Plans were drawn for babies born
To grow this new country
Though fingers torn to plant the corn
For rain we did not see.

A man feels much a greater man
If artisan is he
Our souls were fed by tools in hands,
Erect for family.

The sun shone on our faces,
God shone in the breast
We habituated places
That God had placed to test.

And we were gay, contented
As we worked the day like mules.

We believed we heaven sent-ed
As we toiled with our tools.

At night, the sky awash with stars
White told of past narratives
By firelight he'd paint the sight
Of fights and friendly natives.

He'd paint exotic pictures
Of the red man's size and girth.
We pure quoted scriptures.
Both sides blessed the birth
Blessed Eleanor - his daughter-
And of the countries Christian first.

Some say they saw a future fate
Forged in those flaming embers
This land, the Crown's, we'd consecrate
By our committed members.

A miracle! The flyboat sailed!
On Spicer's navigation.
God was praised and Jesus hailed
We jumped with jubilation!

Our companions thus united!

In a fortified bubble.
We planned Manteo knighted
Negate the native trouble.

With muskets, swords and pointed stakes
Felt safe within, secure
We'd shoot the deer and fish the lakes
With faith we would endure.

But still no drops for soil to slake
Dropped from the clear azure.
No rain to rake for crops to take
Though prayed for by us pure.

We evolved a peaceful Protestant town
Assembled in high humour.
Then a shout of 'Where is Howe?'
We rushed around the rumour.

We rushed to search and called and climbed
Treetops for forty acres
We prodded bush, big bang sticks primed-
Hilltops to bluffs and breakers.

Poor George Howe was found some how
Bought back atop a barrow

His fissog mashed, his body slashed
And porcupined with arrows.

His pin covered figure, disfigured by Wicca
Was a mesh of whip cut welts.
Rusty strands clenched in raw hands
I'd swear hair strands of the Celts.

Oh the panic that befell the camp!
A blizzard bit, devoid of damp
I knew but dared not say aloud-
Red cyclone struck without a cloud.
Panic hit the crowd some more
By clouds of crows with 'Kill' in caw.

No more a place of innocence,
Tranquility was broke.
Vendetta fueled militants
Scoured the Roanoke.

In John White fell a red mist
He bayed for the blood of the brutes.
In his hapless luck and temper twist
They maimed Manteo's troops.

And now no Indian ally

And I foresaw much much worse
And I fret to stay and dally
But to scuttle from the curse.

Ah! The terrors when I shut my lids!
The horrors haunting me
I dreamt the murders of the kids
I craved a boisterous sea.

I begged be off, be to the Bay
But 'twas a big conundrum
As Blue Bill Brown was in the way-
More dread than what I'd run from.

We buried Howe in a shallow shrine-
Dry dirt was heat baked dust.
Belatedly White saw the sign
And signaled a move was a must.

"No!" Said the swine, leant o'er the bow
"This is where thou'll keep!"
"How" said I "is the state o' that boy?"
-"Why, I put him ashore last week!"

White roared the defraud of the declared debt
Then ordered the row to the fort.

I sobbed and begged to the sun had set,
Offered vast awards for transport.

I paid him much a whole years wage
Of a merchant in the city
Whilst in my ears there rang the rage
Of the departing committee.

I foot a fine to that eager swine.
Now I bunked in John White's quarters.
And I spelt the sign that it past the time
To leave these malignant waters.

A rabid rook of Roanoke
Flew round to mocketh me
The goading rook and a boding smoke
Imprisoned me at sea.

The bastard crow with its bastard caw!
It's caws most gross and ribald!
It seared my mind so I sealed my door
With pages ripped from my bible.

I care'th not, not a raindrop fell,
Or of Virginia's christening
For we'd ushered in an utter Hell,

Lured God away from listening.

I saw well enough from my sealed room.
Saw White in his desperation,
Saw the colonies impending doom
Prophesied from my hibernation.

The cursed crow came till I went insane
To squawk along my sill
I ill with pain as it squawked the name
Of the nemesis name of Bill.

John White pleaded every day
'A passage - to replenish stocks!'
And every day the swine said "Nay!
You'll stay here on these rocks!"

I urged speed off for we'd woke the wroth
Of some ungodly djinn.
We'd caused a chasm by the anti Adam.
Took evil to Eden to sin.

Oh dear Lord, let this nightmare cease!
I implore you Christ almighty.
I'll pray all day the demise of the beast
If you'd grease the path to Blighty.

An answering nor'easter gale
Drove us from the cursed coast.
'The Lion' sailed as my prayers prevailed
Upon the Holy Ghost.

Ye Gods, we bobbed like brandy corks
But all my prayers and all my thoughts
Went to repatriating English ports,
To escape that toxic pirate fort
And sail away from stinking tenures.
The swine talked still of stealing ventures.

The weather calmed, sea faired to nicer.
The flyboat neared with Edward Spicer.
I clocked to the noble captains right
Proud on the prow stood Governor White.

Bless be Spicer! Bless his eyes
For taking White to get supplies,
Spicer exposed his unwound neck
To let the Governor board his decks.

I spied White's hex at work again
When the capstan broke and men in pain.
His friendship I began to rue

To see the captains crippled crew.
The crew with broken bones and worse
Care of White and his ebony curse.

Half a crew, no wind blew
Both boats were lagged in loiters.
Lazy, for the spirits knew-
Chastisement for exploiters.

We went from utter idleness
To wild and wet wer-storms
Most sagged in sickened lifelessness
Like dolls in human forms.

Like men morphed into mannequins,
Pus coughed from corrupt lungs.
Like the strangled cut from scaffoldings
With scurvy bloodied gums.

And I could barely hold my quill
These terror'd months returning
For that ghost crow sat upon my sill
And stated I'd be burning.

And still the swine swept salt seas,
Sniffing round for spoils.

Scorned poor shipmates with disease,
The swabs with swollen boils.

With ailing cries the undead scratched
For weeks upon my door.
Morbid magpies sought my stash
Till sighted Blighty's shore.

And men were dead and more were dread
To find some similar fates
And White had fled when Spicer said
He'd lost near half his mates.

I went to bed when I hit my stead
Once passed the city gates.
I sought my bed though through my head
Foreboding fluctuates.

I stayed in bed or prayed in church
And bathed in holy water.
Bed or church sat on a perch
The ghost crow sat in squawker.

Haunt me not, devil bird!
Thou with the glower of Bill.
With thy auburn hair and sadists stare

Sat there on my sill.

Be gone! And come back never more!
You rub me raw with your cursing caw
Your eyes of moss and cinnamon mane,
Your bluish blush as if woad stain...
I wish ye gone! Ye phantom bane!

No cajoling, no reward
Could see me back again on board
Nor Raleigh's title guaranties
Per chance to meet Mephistopheles.

The Painter White was pinched in pain
And daily got more frantic
The war with Spain had squashed his aim
To cross a quick Atlantic.

By and by, over and over and over yet
White to return did try
But Britain lost all her interest,
Found fatter fish to fry…

Cold dread sweats here in my bed.
I petrified at stuff crow said
Solidified from toe to head-

A screaming statue cast in lead.

In dreams we be an ant colony
Tortured by teal Titan
A fiend from Greek mythology,
An age this vision frightened.

-Bills blue head, not ears but wings instead
Trampled by his giant tread
And everywhere we hid Bill sees us
Replacing his with the viz of Jesus.
Bicey eyes were stone and starey
My antenna'd eyes forever wary
I dream him flapping, fornicating Mary!

How to halt rapes of the Virgin
Whilst seeping sanity was blurring?

Heaven weeping whilst I sleeping
Imagining the ghastly reaping,
The harvesting and then the eating
Of the souls that we'd forsaken
By the freak that we had taken…

Oh blasphemy! Oh heresy!
These acts I see are haunting me!

I pray him dead across the sea
To perish and to set me free.

Good Lord what had we gone and done?
I'd burn for bringing Satan's son
I fret. But return for my redemption?
I need survive, top up my pension.

Then Liz –Beth called, to serve the war
Rich men could pay. She'd arm the poor.
And still the ghost crow at my door
Squawked hateful sounds. More and more.

More and more crows murderous caw
From months to years outside my door
Louder now than he before.
Foul demon from cruel days of yore.

Too rich. No wish to join the militia.
I'd fight not Parma's army.
A Spanish pike could'na prick my psych
Like a petrifying journey.

So I paid most of my pension
To stay at home, flat broke.
Twisting at night in tension

About the Roanoke.

I twisted, nor no business.
No income from my stores.
And I damned to hell as witness
The desecration of those foreign shores.

With Philips Armada firmly beat,
Ships released from off the fleet.
Who should come upon my street?
He with planned new expedition.
White rose me from my chamber prison.

I rose composed a holy quest
Rose for my financier.
A sainthood waited – I to be blessed
When slayed the necromancer.

We sailed in spring in 'The Hopewell'
The name was apt for White.
My spirit soared as parallel
Sailed Spicer in 'Moonlight"

A fortune Raleigh personally paid-
To impress haughty heir of Boleyn.
I sought return to crusade.

White to contact kin.

Three. Fraught. Years.
Shear panic, shedding tears.
Pacing, pleading, every day got harder.
The missing leader. Father. Grandfather.
Refused return to stock their larder.

The stress was mighty on White's health.
A shadow now of his former self.
Coughing, sniffing, limping, aching.
His heart three years of straining, breaking.
Bright eyed again as we were making
Waves to weigh with fresher hope.
Wending back to Roanoke.

The return was mild. The weather fairer.
'Cept detours for our ships to plunder.
I was wired to right our error
White gaunt gripped in hopeful wonder.

Gripped in hopeful wonder,
But he anxious and irate.
For the Pirates pursued plunder,
John White could hardly wait.
His people all? Or torn asunder?

Keen to find out what their fate.

And then we spied a plume of smoke!
Two rowboats rowed to Roanoke
Brave Edward led, who on top form
Saw he not the sudden storm.

Catastrophe! What alchemy
Had mixed this evil gale?
We yelled to turn the tragedy.
Yelled to no avail.

The sea was like a living snake
In wreathing, writhing twist.
It coiled and dipped and in its wake
There sprayed a blinding mist.

A cloaking blinding mist, I wist
It enveloped in its covers.
Revealed when neared much as I feared
Drowned Spicer and six others.

As Spicer shown his sodden grave
I sagged in sickened swound.
I wished it White in swallowed wave,
For'd tarnished those around.

White pressed proceed and Cocke agreed,
Time not for terse bereaving.
To land at noon, to flute the tune -
 'Greensleeves.' Perhap' a receiving.

More merry English tunes were struck,
To tempt those with nerves a seared.
But White again was out of luck
For not a soul appeared.

Nor not a soul came to our shore
For cannons echoed blast
So walked we did to where before
Three years before had past.

We walked the old familiar way,
No man dared speak a word
For dank and dismal felt that day.
The fort…
Sat a blackbird.

The settlement forsaken,
The dwellings were dismantled.
White screamed loud in desperation
And all of us stood rankled.

"Where art thee girls? Where did ye go?
Lord pity on the pious!"
There shadowed him a spectral....
CROw, "where AT!- Oh AnaNias?"

What was this sign carved on a pine?
This cryptic code of CRO?
Bedamn my beard for that blackbird
It cruel appeared to know.

It locked on me its callous eyes.
I startled stiff in fright.
It conjured blustered bruising skies
To drain me all my fight.

I drained of every inch of fight-
Bled from that feathered phantom.
I fled in throttled fearful flight
To the 'Hopewell's' sanctum.

The clouds were crows with boiling wings
And thunder rolls cawed hateful things.
The wind whipped rigging sang a song
As we dipped and crashed and bobbed along.
'Greensleeves' the cables crooked tune.

Ghastly green I fell in swoon.

Miles, sweet miles when I awoke
Relief! As miles from Roanoke.
We skated still on sea churned foam
But sweet Lord - we headed home.

The men pressed home, or mutiny.
It shattered John White's soul.
He slumped in distressed scrutiny,
Sucked dry by squandered goal.

Shattered as so near, so far.
He'd die a broken wreck.
I'll sit at home with chill memoirs
To save my snake-bit neck.

'Tis Satan and that stormy sea
Keeps me inside my gown
I'll venture for not any fee.
Not leave my London Town.

I'll pray but stay here in my cot.
Pray God sharp shoots his bolt!
Pray God would lightning strike the rot-
Forgives the missions fault.

I'll pray away my weakness
Pray all evil we'd accessed
Did'na strew a blanket bleakness
On that virgin land out west.

Book 5
Matwau Rising

Narrator-
Hanging from her hairy tree
That she herself did plant
The folk took little notice
Of the wretch's wretched rant.

The memory of wee Agnes
In Girvan was always vague,
Not one recalled the first one
From the witch that called the plague.

No one recalled her first boy.
Her sibling and her son
Who'd inherited the spinach eye,

Strange skin of cerulean.

For Agnes was expectant
When escaped from Sawney's lair.
Had had her fathers giant child
With his ginger giant hair.

The babe was blue, quadruple
But a spit for Sawney's hue
And so berserk and brutal
That she'd hidden him from view.

Six years she'd hidden William
Who was then more twice her size
Then packed him off to London-
Husband, purse and in disguise.

Her ploughman paid four seamen
To take Bill out to sea
To sail away that demon
On any ship - to set her free.

A decade that she'd lived in dread,
A return of Blue Bill riled.
Ten recovered, then she'd said
"I'll have another child"

A decade gone and Sawney done
They'd hauled the menace down.
She'd cherished on her sandy son
And hoped the ginger drowned.
For she reviled her first born child
That horror Blue Bill Brown.

1589-
Summer

Tom Smart-
"Now Governor Dare,
Let us be clear
In sane and sober eye.
If we stay here it is our fear
That we will surely die"

"We're out of powder, low on chowder
Chained to try to farm,
You pious have your wives to ride.
We have Madam Palm"

"For two full years we tried to rear,
But blisters, boils and bunions
And backs a bent enough to tear

A bag o' bloody onions."

"Our backs all hurt through constant work
From toiling in the heat.
And though you might have fun at night
We landed hand or seat"

"And while you pray and make the hay
We missing, one a month!
If we stay we're premier prey,
Packaged for the hunt."

"We're frontline as we work the field!
No ammo, aching balls.
You grind behind your wooden shield
Of pointy pine tree walls"

"We have no shot and woe begot
Those stranded on their own.
Frustration felt as we in melt
To till this dusty loam."

"I sussed the game, frustrate Spain's aim
"By loading here with thugs...
It's lack of Dames and rain for grain.
We're bursting! Drained like mugs."

"You zealots have your girls or God,
You think We lewd and dirty!
But we think abstinence is odd,
Agreed all of us thirty."

"Us thirty are to live like they.
How nature had intended!
We'll root as in the Native way,
Root Manteo's wenches"

"We choose to crude - not civil,
To naked, nay attire.
We'll be fulfilled and root until
Returns the bloody liar."

"Where is the bloody liar White?
Where has your law Pa gone?
'S' not what we signed, this life of shite
Procured it by a con"

"We bought here on a promise!
Now we shadowed with White's hex.
We been gullible and novice
And denied the fairer sex"

"This bloody drought and us without
No dainty one to hold.
This lands severe, unless you're queer
And not a sniff o' gold."

"The lack of skin to kiss, caress
We cannot work or focus!
For we are men and we possess
Throbbing red hot pokers…"

Ananias Dare-
"Civility! Calm ye your vibe!
Upon this council meet!
Those who choose Manteo's tribe
I pray you take a seat"

"I pray ye quickly find the Christ
Or be ye unprotected!
Leave the fold and pay the price
Ye devil lust infected."

"Manteo'll hold you in low esteem
At best you'll be guest slaves.
Be celibate! And drop your dream
Of rutting savage maids."

"Be celibate! And celebrate
Good hard honest toil.
Then you'll enter heavens gate!
Reward for staying loyal."

"You'll have your fun- with angels
After you have died!
Unbolt celestial stables
For what you've been denied."

"Just hold on till your life is gone,
Forget all earthly pleasures!
Your muscle pains are for sweet gains
To take cherubic treasures."

"If we divide we halve our force.
I'll tell thee Smart the gob.
If leave the fort you'll set your course
To ruin by your knob.
Hold your horse and be the source-
An inspiring modern Job…"

Winter.

Ananias-
"We're down to forty fighting men

Since all the rest have split.
But lo, we have no sex pests left,
To God the best submit."

Eleanor-
"I fear him! Ananias dear
I spy him 'yond those trees!
I see his carni-vorous stare
It fears my blood to freeze."

Ananias-
"We must pray harder Eleanor!
To invite the Holy Ghost.
The spirits shy as secular
Sods still at this post."

Eleanor-
"I fear him for he floods my dreams
I'm owned. I am his goods!
I fear the blue. Fear what he'll do-
Fear he's watching from the woods.
I fear he tread toward my bed
To claim his chamber goods."

Ananias-
"We'll construct a wooden church!

And That will cure our woe.
The Lord will sight from cloudy perch
And gifts God will bestow!"

Eleanor-
"I dread him, Ananias Dare.
In sleep He press me close.
His fingers fondle me down there,
He haunts this heathen post."

Ananias-
"Tis 'cause of unbelievers!
The cause of all this fuss,
The famine, thirst and fevers.
Gods turned his back on us!"

Eleanor-
"I don't believe he's dead, Dare
From snippets that I've heard.
I hear him in my nightmare
Shape shifting to a bird"

Ananias-
"We'll spend more time in praising,
Worship is the cure.
By His grace amazing

We'll survive this epic tour"

Eleanor-
"I'm ravaged by this rancid rook
Who rapes me every night!
It is the savage Scottish cook
Transforming after flight."

Ananias-
"Be calm Eleanor. Calm ye may
Upon this Christmas eve
Profane ye not on Gods day,
Your safe if you believe!"

Eleanor-
"A hideous ginger jackdaw
I'm fret and weak to fight.
He consumes me like a ruined whore
Succumbing to his might."

Ananias-
"Sleep my dear. Virginia's there.
You'll wake her with your shout!
Be not afraid, stout palisade
Would stop the Scottish lout."

Eleanor-

"I spied his eyes along our trip.
A sexual pervert!
Staring off my blouse and slip,
Thinking off my skirt!"

Ananias-
"No more Eleanor, with that thought
You'll tempt Old Nick to hear.
We're safe, us three, within this fort
I pray you lose your fear…"

Narrator-
Upon the Ships arrival
Bill packed himself a pack
To insure for his survival,
Stole cheese off the kitchen rack.

The sailors trussed him in a skiff,
Marooned him on the beach.
Skillfully he scaled the cliff
Planned vengeance he'd to teach.

The heir felt not a twinge of fear
Amongst the watchful trees.
Was not alone as crows had flown
When whiffed his moulding cheese.

There he found, crow surrounded
By warriors of Chief Wanchese
Who revered him on the spot as some
Strange God from overseas.

He was brought before their warlock
Who had prophesied the word-
A flame haired one of spirit stock
Who'd mastered the black bird.

The witch doctor – Sugnog
Sycophantically purred
A glorifying dialogue,
Extolled the coppered bird.

They sat him high on palanquin
Dressed him in feathered cloak.
Worshipped by the Algonquin
Around the Roanoke.

They hailed Ahone, ray of sun,
Huge halo of red hair.
His hair shone like the setting sun
His skin blue frosted air.
The murder always followed on

For crumbs of dairy share.

He made the most of all the praise,
Lapped up all the licking.
Prophesied the end of days.
Said raptures clock was ticking.

The chief that travelled London
Did not need too much persuading.
The sun child quoth 'It hath begun!
With start o' White's invading.'

Said of White men-
"Dey da demon scum!
Dey come do take thy land!
Ift you'll arm n'give I's some
I's makes a holy stand!"

Bill hand picked a jihadi band.
He picked the most suspicious.
Most religious mostly and
The bloody mostly vicious."

Those obeyed the things he said
Those cruel with bovine nature,
Those who needed to be led,

Those who'd bolst his stature.

He orchestrated Howe's attack,
The ambush on the river.
One brave, Chogan, held him back
From eating out Howe's liver.

That night a squaw, in anguished yaw,
Staggering and shrieky
Screamed a mortifying roar-
Screamed murder in her teepee.

Chogan's scalp had fateful flap
His head was almost severed.
No eyes, crow claws stuffed in eye gap.
Slack mouth stuffed black with feathers.

No trial, nor any summoning,
For Sugnog staid their hands.
For he'd foretold the coming
Of red thunder in their lands.

He foretold but fearful worried
And did not know what to do
For the sun child was now sullied
For he'd broke the tribes taboo.

Taboos were broke and oft' was stoke
The fires of holy battle.
Victory foretold in smoke.
Heathens merely chattel.

One a week they'd stalk and slay
Settlers, other clans.
His gang obliged in angst obey
To aid his predator plans.

They soon knew what he doing
When he dragged mauled meat away.
For soon his crew were chewing
Off the flesh from off men prey.

Sugnog saw of his mistake
And voiced it to the cowed-
The sun-sky prophet was a fake...
Found Sugnog disemboweled.

Bill went to squat the shaman's hut
And fostered all the hype.
Carrion crows kept up the guise,
Their wage was human tripe.

Step by step he sought to climb
Further up the tower.
Now a rung below the prime.
He had the shaman's power.

And whilst the crops were withered,
Most the tribe had start to starve
He acknowledged wonder wizard
For he'd conjured meat to carve.

His holy gang of slayers
Weren't the only players fed.
Soothsayers in compliance
Withal fed upon his dead.

Sated Mystics spread the myth-
His blood deeds came to lore.
His enterprise excessive with
Mountains of pain and gore.

And all the time he authorised-
'Dis sanctified n'right!
Dese meals are merely infidels
For us appetite!'

A sickness swept o'er the tribe,

The flux cut half them down.
Those survived were those subscribed
To the will o' Blue Bill Brown.

They thought him More a prophet Lord,
Their belly's he kept filling.
Their pox was cured when he procured
Cheese dosed with penicillin.

The doubters lay like skeletons-
Famished, ulcered, thin.
His band of rogues had healthy tones
With glowing golden skin.

They glowed in only outer shell
Inside them growled black beast.
As like the crows that sought the smell,
More savage every feast.

They glowed in their appearance
But their eyes were black with sin.
Steeped dark with their adherence
To the spite that dwelt within.

They only glowed with close-ed eyes
And close-ed cruel lips…

For they'd oculus of crows in guise,
Teeth filed to pointed tips.

Wanchese lost mostly all his grip,
Too weak to wield his lever.
No cheese to cure did pass ill lip,
Struck down with yellow fever.

And in a lavish ceremony,
Kuffars round them ailing
'Matwau' –mortal enemy-
Their messiah named at naming.

Matwau! Spoke in fearful awe
By menaced unbelievers.
Echoed by the murders caw
To taunt those struck with fevers.

Matwau turned his twenty team
To live a year nomadic.
Pursued his dream of his regime,
Now hunting here sporadic.

They crossed unto to the mainland
To conquer, in canoes
To wrought an utter wasteland

To rape, to kill, abuse.

They terrorized the native stock,
Subdued with terrorism.
Expanded his expanding flock
By bowed evangelism.

They found a camp of negroes
And slaughtered all but three.
The three with savage egos
Who joined the company.

And in recruit from other tribes.
Those sloughed in decadence.
Chose Indians with vicious vibes,
Some seven Secotans.

Six settlers too who'd evil view.
Each with a villain story.
Who'd fled the fort to join the crew
Led by Charlie Flory.

Thirty seven men at arms,
Marauders. Matwau leading.
Terrorizing native farms.
Ten squaws were farmed for breeding.

Terrorizing other tribes
Who praised or paid a tax.
To stay alive they paid this bribe
Or suffered ghastly acts.

On their return with Matwau grown
As big as the biggest brave
With high desire to seize the throne,
To show Wanchese his grave.

Wanchese was fading, dying
But he still held off his homage.
His deity denying
Held back the healing stale fromage.

Near Yuletide and with smatter'd snow,
Old chieftain a la mort.
Chief Matwau had designs to go
Attack the settlers fort.

He painted all his warriors red,
Their faces Corvus black
To fill his foe of frigid dread
In the night attack.

Naked painted warriors
Tooled up to pointed teeth
They filed behind their glorious
Anointed Lord of death.

Cruel cannibals swarmed the silent grove.
Midnight, Christmas Eve
They stunned and beat and roped and drove
Pale pilgrims to the sea.

Matwau's attack supremely timed
As streamed the stockades pass.
No settler had a weapon primed,
All posed in praise en masse.

The screams were sweet off of the meat,
Music from the larder.
Matwau stiff for he could sniff
Sheer terror for his ardor.

His ardor quenched by sordid vice
His cult bayed he a sage.
The settlers scattered scared as mice.
The clan bayed at his rage.
Bayed at buggered Tony Cage
Who'd dared to bare a crucifix,

Shredded by the lunatic.

And it was a hellish sight
The things Bill did to him that night.
In strange religious ritual..
Hailed dripping visceral.
As he hailed for killing, rutting
Someone desperate was woodcutting.

No musket primed but carved a sign,
-Tom Stevens etched a pine
Prayed-in time- the **CRO**w **ATO**(A)**N**e.
-Carved Matwau caused this crime

CROw **MAT**wau **O**n a m**AN**ic fit
Twin minds a hanging by a thread
Blue skin was smeared in blood and shit,
Two hours took till Tony dead
Whilst Tom scratched pines by fires lit.
'Fore found his message back re- read
Tom prayed redress by '**CRO**' he writ.

Humming hymns to hacked off limbs
-Festivities aborted
In replace of their saviours face

Was Hells flesh face Bill sported.

Caught off guard at Christmas,
Every settler bound.
Sculling past the isthmus,
O'er the Pamlico sound.
The beatings but a litmus
Test from He who newly crowned.

Book 6
The Fears of Eleanor Dare

1591

Eleanor-
"Please smother dear Virginia,
Ananias, grant me that.
Before It takes, begins the
Render of her fat.
Roped I cannot end her!
Ananias! Grant me that!"

"Before It boils and eats her
Let us have a last embrace.
I'll tell her that I love her.
And I'd love to take her place"

"We've failed and now let's end her
For I cannot stand her hurt.
Now! I fear I will incur
The wrath of that pervert!"

Ananias-
"Eleanor have faith again,
Escaped some of us, seven.
And if we cannot get away
I'll see thee both in heaven."

"White will come a smiting-
Restore the symmetry.
Disinfect he all this blighting.
On his return with infantry."

Eleanor-
"I cannot, Ananias Dare
And will not share your faith!
If less in grovel, more aware
We'd more of us be safe!"

"Faith's not helped, has bought us harm!
I wish you'd change your tack!
Matwau's eaten half your arm!
You pray God grows it back??"

Ananias-
"I'm drained, my wife. Faith quenches fear.
My life is almost spent.
I'm sorry to have bought you here
Sorry you'll not repent."

"I hope there be an after life!
For there I'll make amends
Hope you lose your fear, my wife
And prayer pays dividends."

Eleanor-
"Oh I fearful Ananias!
 I'd prefer if I were food.
And keep your useless prayers
For I'm raped to boost Its brood.
It's peeling back my layers
Till I'm crushed and coarse and crude."

Spring

Eleanor-
"And now you're gone, my husband!
My darling daughter too.
It sautéed with your pious blood and
Made Virginia stew."

"My darling little daughter!
I swear I'll make It pay!
I'll debt settle for your slaughter.
Going to gut the grim gourmet."

"Now always moving, moves away
This caravan of woe.
Not three nights we stop and stay
Then on our way to go."

"In blazing sun or searing snow
In pain and injury
Dragged through the sleet with bleeding feet
Each move a misery."

"Gasping, parched, we forced to march,
Cracked ground in summer scorch.
It put to torch the towns It crossed
That refused to swing around."

"We marched grass spikes of winter frost.
Much more collapsed, were frozen, lost.
I watch them fall and eaten raw,
Watched friends raked by rancid claw.
Watched dead bodies turn and toss
As crows inside jostled, thrust
To dine on grist below the crust."

"They snatch, It's zealous cronies,
To offer, on a skewer.
It blessed at sickened ceremonies
For meat that It procured."

"It blessed and praised and sits upraised
On Its throne of bones.
They chant and dance around It crazed,
Dance around the towns they razed
Intoning to the doomed ones groans"

"Taut skins are tanned for wigwams,
It makes me scrub clean skulls.
Now I ache, tied to a stake
As now I'm on parole.
For this mistake of tried escape
It hammers my every hole."

"I've stitched a human mantle-
I'm so cold, tied to this hitch.
It's binds bite at my ankle
As It treats me as Its bitch."

"Always on, always West,
A waters winding track.
To where we stop, to where It blessed
By tribe Pocoughtronack."

"Here they made It welcome.
Here they're similar kinds.
It'll turn their town to bedlam
For It soaks absorbent minds."

"Lo! And so, not one year on
To see what It inflicted!
It fuels fake fervent men in fawn,
Perfervid elevated.
To see it so and still they go
And hold It venerated?"

"To see them all still worship It?
It's back tracked them primeval.
Their village turned a hellish pit

Since Its 'divine' arrival."

"Season melts to seasons,
Melt to diabolic years.
Matwau's manic legions
Itch to spread Its holy fears."

"So we away, scatter wide Its seed,
For Matwau's sexual sating.
For more to breed, for It decreed
A menu change for mating."

"Each day all thoughts are suicide!
But I'll press on, stay strong.
As all but eight of us have died
And one needs right the wrong."

"Now goes Lizzie Viccars,
Rosie, Emmie Merrimoth.
Defiled by queues of rippers
Raped and stripped, tipped in the broth."

"The four last children clench I close,
They shaken by each scream.
As each taken by King Crow
It tears my very seam."

"Lord forgive! Those timid kids!
I corse with liquid pain.
Squealing sounds as slaughtered pigs.
Their yells drill in my brain."

"I must keep calm and quiet
To survive this Armageddon.
Complicit and compliant
Mind and soul I'll seek to deaden."

"It made me eat the flesh of men!
On pain of being shredded!
I'm but a beast kept in a pen
I've fell. Twas what I've dreaded!"

"Ananias!
 Husband of little lumen!
I need help to stay my sense
To help me stay still human.
I need help prop my defense!
Help me ride this sick offense.
Ease my tension, my suspense
In Its pressured presence
Help regain my draining essence!"

"Defend me Ananias, and soothe my sanity.
Your presence is a golden glimpse
Of strength and sympathy."

"We've stopped our roams like nomads.
Found this cavern. Now Its lair.
I fear Its ginger gonads,
Please sustain me, Mr. Dare!"

"You who but a shadow
But my only consolation.
You wisp as smoke tobacco.
Scant relief from rapine raven."

"You shimmered haze on cavern wall
Who dances with the lantern.
You I miss above them all
You who only can turn
Foul funk and awe for what's in store…"

"I dream of thee an ivory buck
With I a white bucks mate.
Free from the fear and full of love
Not fettered, full of hate."

"I see you when I shut my eyes

My glorious antlered stag
Deer Ananias in disguise-
Distraction from Its nauseous shag"

" I forced to squeeze Its stinking arse
Fake moan, lest I be cut-
I'd dream of softly scented grass
With thee- in forest rut."

"I forced to stroke Its ice cold hide-
'Fore every form of vice
Strange skin as in indigo dyed
Vile skin of sapphired ice."

"Its day is Monday-Moonday.
Where clan kneel for Its advice.
Full rising moon all fawn and pray
Then gut some sacrifice."

"It dictates Its deeds on human skin!
That skin is consecrated..
They task bleak sagas in a spin,
It's deeds exaggerated."

"Its word is spread through fearful skies!
Its 'miracles' are basic lies.

None dare differ, fear reprisals.
Still more revere the wing-ed idol."

"I fear the crescent, pumpkin moon,
Fear noon and dusk and dawn
It magnified as I ballooned
With Matwau's bastard spawn."

"I hate it! Hate this foreign thing!
That grows inside of me!
Know it spawn of blue Crow King,
Collapsed humanity.

"Just I survived. I, no other.
I who lives in chains.
Matwau said I'd suffer
So much more than labor pains
If abort the clone of 'Mamma',
Ordered Agnes be her name."

"It ordered me, dead husband!
To bear Its child a she!
If not got what It customed
It come chow down on me!"

"I fearist now my fathers dead.

I dreamt him in the nether.
I bound. Cannot cave in my head-
Unite us all together."

"Still dream of I a snowy deer
Free! In a misty park
I free the fiend and free the fear,
I free this filthy dark."

"The Chesapeake, I think I know
Location of this cave.
I'll scratch another hint in stone
Chance soldiery to save."

"I'll carve in rocks more clues for
Justice be delivered.
Incriminating Matwau-
The woe crow cunt hath triggered."

"It is a she! So I survive!
Although I do not live.
This babe might save. For her I'll drive
On. And love I'll give."

"And now she born much I forlorn
To think the thoughts I had

Though she his, she most adored,
My antidote to sad."

"A darling little parcel,
She knows not this be wrong
To munch on the metatarsal
Of a squaw it'd once belong."

"I fearful of her future,
Fear her ferocious sire
Fear I'll not long can suture
Of It's debased desire."

"But it seems she is the prized.
Heads all Its other runts.
Not too much that she chastised
For disrespectful stunts."

"I refuse to be Its factory!
Though cherish I my tot.
I've damaged what's inside of me
And sterilized my twat."

"I'll civilize she that's mine,
And shun Its other brood
Won't add another to the nine.

My solitary feud."

"I will not fall compliant
Like the other mothers seem.
I'd die with my defiance
Than expand Its horror team."

"Now Agnes six, exploring-
Though try tie her in the crèche
As the caverns sights abhorring,
I try disguise the human flesh."

"She plays with bones as if they're dolls
An innocence heart breaking.
I shield her from what It involves
Me in and my degrading."

"I shield her from Its followers
Who skulk about the cave
The fiends who are the swallowers
Of sermons most depraved."

"I tell her all the screams are songs
Of spirits who've released.
Soothe her as these hateful wrongs
Seem only to increase."

"Now a little older, a lot harder to protect.
Matwau calls her 'Mamma'
She's sex interest to his sect.
I got some dead for what I said-
Sliced from arse to ear!
Three warriors who approached her bed.
Dead, when went too near."

"Mamma! Goliath constant calls
A girl who's age is nine.
Repulsed! My skin doth crawl!
It's crossed the bottom line"

"I'll kill It if I get the chance.
If conquer can my quiver.
I'll stab if not in terror trance
And give it to the giver"

"But Lord I am so frightened
And I fear I'd miss heart goal.
Please make me more enlightened
How to best the beryl troll."

"When It nears I shudder - shake.
 -I am useless scared and riled

But Its murder plans I still will make
To protect my feral child."

"She's to survive if I'm to drive
In It a yard of steel.
The cult will kill then both we will
Be but another meal."

"I implore you God – or thee my spouse
Deer Ananias hear?
Help me with the succubus
When right the time is near."

"Tis the slightest compensation
When It disappears for days
But I'm guarded by Its ravens
Who do all that It obeys."

"They sit and guard the entrance
And watch with much malaise.
They watch with all resemblance
Of dun devils in their gaze."

"I fear them, demon avians!
Fear my eyes they'll peck!
Black hearted feathered aliens,

Its petrifying pets."

"Way they strut to guard the brothel.
Way they root in people offal.
Pickings dripping off their beak.
The sounds they make as if they speak."

"Whore! Whore!' The chorus caws
'Whore!' Cave echoed chimes.
'Why for I is?' I asks them this.
'This!' Repeats the mimes."

"Can I go on much further?
With this murder, bloody murder!
My life gets only harsher
As I've lost my inner armour.
I'm in constant bloody filth!
But I'll not just die a martyr
I've this testimony to spilth.
And I'll not be dead and rested
Till I have the beast arrested."

"And these streams of screaming victims
From a multitude of tribes
Are stuffed into the pigpens
Then they snuffed. I tan their hides."

"I tan their skin but from within
I pray their souls to glide.
I pray for they to find a way
The peace they've been denied."

"The murder agitated!
The family runs for cover!
Six assassinated!
For It feels Its hanging mother!"

"Oh Ananias please protect,
It wrenched Ness to Its lair!
Tis a first I see It wept
When It wept into her hair."

"It is so fearful sickening
To see It slumped and slobbering.
The atmosphere is thickening
The menace growing, hovering
Its odour overpowering!
And now green eyes are glowering
About for a devouring!
Can't spit, my spittle's souring.
I'm so anxious with alarm!"

"Still It calls her 'Mamma'
I fear It cause her harm!
 I twisted with the trauma
At Its 'Mamma' nursing drama!
Slim hope It's killed by karma.
So her chance is with her charm."

"I thank ye spirit intervention!
But I'm shaken to the core.
I know of Its intention
If Agnes blossoms more.
I torn apart in tension
Predicting what's in store."

"I've got to get her out of here-
Pay for her escape.
I'll approach the Buccaneer
To try to stop her rape."

"An', I so miss Miss Virginies
But I do love little Agnes.
Bribed Bright by bags of Guineas
To renew his pirate practice"

"I've promised John a fortune
To secure Ness a release.

My ransom buys his Whore Town
If he'd ship her overseas."

Narrator-
Johnny Bright was set alight
His treachery uncovered.
His torched remains were torn by kite
Dog, rat and crab and buzzard.

An English boat was spied to float
Into Chesapeake bay.
Matwau slit five English throats
To scare the ship away.

In agonizing torture
Bright spilled his guts- then told.
Matwau sent a searcher,
For Bright lit with thinks of gold.

Eleanor-
"Oh dark despair! I shot with woe,
So close was a reprieve.
I'd packed a sack for Ness to go
And told her time to leave."

"It made me watch the sinking mast

Sink the sad horizon.
With that ship all hope had passed.
My soul it start to siphon."

"It sucked me of my marrow
Till I could not draw a breath.
Agnes stopped Its arrow
To halt my wished for death."

"She threw her body over mine
Cold challenged Matwau's will.
Her tiny frame had paused designs
Of Its lust to kill."

"She thought she'd done a favour!
My save from gallows rope.
But now I seek my saviour
For I've lost all of my hope."

"Yet years go by I still deny
The primate I've become.
You deer ghost is what I rely
Lest I be dull and dumb."

"I rely on you, dead husband
As Agnes disappears.

I don't know what she does and
It fills me full of fears.
I try. I'm weak. I cannot stand.
I fear my ending nears."

"My sleep disturbed by hard-core haunts,
Now Agnes is pubescent.
I fear It of Its obscene wants,
Motives of pure putrescence."

"I fear It figures fuck her.
Like It forms and fucks her mind
I'm out of tricks to deter-
It. I still am chained, confined."

"Ananias' apparition-
I dream ye in my head.
Deer, Dare -be more than haunting vision
And send spirits from the dead!"

"Summon souls to liquidate!
Time ticks for teenage Agnes!
Tell fathers ghost participate-
Come crush cruel cobalt canis!"

"Sixteen years!

I've cried a creek of hopeless tears.
I've ground smooth my survival gears,
Fostering my phobic fears,
Forced to every degradation
I'm sick of my fake adulation.
I beg now for my one salvation,
Save Agnes from this aberration."

"I offer I as sacrifice!
Oh spirits listen, please!
Save Her from Its monstrous vice-
It's mind of fire, it's heart of ice!
Deer ghost! Dear God!
My life for she's.
I've so much fear...
Oh Dare! My deer...
 Dear God...
Please..."

Part 3

.

Book 7
Copper Pots at Ritanoe

From' The White Doe'
by Sallie Southall Cottons -1901

"Trusting the crow, his food and his fiefdom
Wresting a tribute from forest and sea
A chilling forecast of doom in the future
Daunts his bent spirit by freedom made bold
Far o'er the wildwood he roams at his pleasure
The fierce brawny red man is king of the wold"

"The fierce brawny red man is king of the wold"

"The fierce brawny red man is king of the
wold!"

Friday 1st November 1605. London

Narrator-
The King of England's jam ring hot,
A silk plug rushed and teased in.
The Pygmy leaked the powder plot
-Of explosive treason

Pucker valve and Parliament
Both threatened with exploding.
Shaking in incontinence,

James trembled with foreboding

All season nighttime sweating cobs
In gore tormented dreams
Nay dreams of crazed catholic mobs
But Sawney and the Beans.

James feared them more than Jesuits-
A dead fearful family.
Now Guido Fawkes had forced in corks
To spare shamed agony.

James squeezed both cheeks to stem the leaks
And forced himself to stand
And prayed nay smelt the portents, felt
In a distant land

Same themes were dreamed by Don Louis
Ne' Opechancanough
Who'd lived a Spanish missionary
'Fore slaughtering the monks

Erased eight priests at Ajacan
For frightful premonitions
Signed the signal to attack and
Slay pale expeditions

His superstitions would not cease
For over three decades
With omen eyes they'd be no peace
Till vanquished ghost crusades

That troubled chief of Kiskiak
With haunting muddled visions
Was charged with healing Gaia's crack-
Repair rough earthly rhythms

The evil beat felt not around
That bright autumnal day
By Manteo in his peaceful town
Two hundred miles away

That worthy man felt not bad vibe
As blessed he bride and groom,
Blessed by all his Christian tribe
In his loved long room

His loved longhouse two stories high
Set further for expansion,
English built to typify
Raleigh's Durham mansion

Manteo still so struck with awe
Twice seeing London's glory
Constructed it in miniature
In his territory

His Croat town it proudly stood
And 'twas a glorious thing
With sturdy walls of stone and wood
Good governed by that King

That awe struck King that oversaw
Much intermingling
Twixt English and indigenous-
The cream and honey skinned

Their offspring now were getting wed.
This day was Smart's son Jim.
Mild Manteo stood and said
'Festivities begin!'

Ex city folk blessed every day,
The fathers they'd become
They'd blessed the day they'd sailed away
And left their city slum

The guests danced naked in the sun

Around their children dancing
Kicking dust to the wedding drum
With the dust devil whirls entrancing

And the feast was fine and plied with rum
Fermented from blue berries
The families blessed what had become-
United, fed and merry.

Manteo sat south of the totem pole,
Joy watched the jamboree
For the dance was droll round the totem pole
From his adopted family

Grinned Richard Kemme with his team of ten
With dancing wives, all three
Fourteen a hoot when Mylette's flute
Tooted Kemme's with wobbling knees

John Starte danced like he rowed a raft
Well fortified with brew
The chuffed chief laughed this romping craft
-Six sons rowed an air canoe

The brothers Wyles jumped imaginary styles,
John Farre swum in the air.

The craziness of the colonists dance
Caused a cordial affair

It caused more mirth seeing Mizenher
Pick fairy fruit off a phantom tree
But when Micah spied the visitor
Gripped they their families

The thrum of the drums fell silent
Both flutes both ceased to blow
Music in the air displaced by despair,
Whoops were replaced with woe

Came a naked wizened visitor
As old as old could be
She twanged like the strings of the fiddler
As she gatecrashed the ceremony

Her walnut face most sinister
She shaped like a tree bark shard
Her eyes two clouds that sliced the crowd
Though her summit 'twere hardly a yard

No tooth pegged in the hags eat hole
But her twang had the force of a lash
She thicked the blood of the stoutest soul

When her voice whipped a lightning flash

'Beware! Beware the Wendigo!'
The witch bawled to the wedding.
No man tried seize her, seize their chance
For her sightless glare held them in a trance
Infectious fear out from her spreading

Her croaking cry stopped dead the dance
And the day turned dull and chilly
And the tribe stood shaken in a trance
As the witch screeched on more shrilly

'The Wendigo comes and with it comes
Woe!
Go! Try to escape the Wendigo!
'Neath its indigo skin lies a beast within
There never is nor never has been…
A foe so cruel as the Wendigo!'

The monarch Manteo, and he alone
Tried silencing the cackling crone
The crone still spat though he held her tight
As the end of the day bled into night

'The omens there! That there crow!

Tis a shadow of the Wendigo!
Heed these warning signs of Woe
Go! It comes! The Wendigo!'

The wedding fell silent, in a silent pause
And the only sounds sounding
Were distant caws
And Jim the groom and Tala, his bride
Anxiously looked for a place to hide

Twas as if the evening had a sense of shift-
Splitting the earth's spirit essence
And the wedding guests started off to drift
With the draining luminescence

And a deathly pall settled on the crowd
And the crickets all stopped crikin
And every heart beat beat out loud
With terrored timely ticking

Every heart beat the grimest theme
To the little witch conductor
Which chilled the skin with her every scream
Of warning she did utter

A multitude of mystic whistles

Iced the blood of the guests much more
A pause 'fore a hail of missiles
From the cloudless sky did pour

It was a deadly deluge
Of dart and stone and spear
And the revellers seeking refuge
Ran random filled with fear

Manteo willed boost he bolder-
Try shield his tribe from harm.
A spear loosed drilled his shoulder
As he steered retreat to the barn

The injured chief saw his peoples grief,
Pure panic in them surged
For leisurely, nay dreamily
From the woods the wolves emerged

Many guests fell and the many all killed,
Assassinated lazily
For the wolves had the town encircled
As they closed in tranquilly

 They moseyed behind their commander-
Who twenty tall hands high,

Who's wolf pelt looked much grander
On a trunk like the morning sky

Manteo stood with his sentries
With his back to his Manor House door.
The wolf horde arrayed against these
Pitiful band of four

Enemy archers bent their bows
And set their arrows aiming
And every house 'cept the longhouse doused
With kindled arrows flaming

 The Wendigo removed its pelt
And likewise did it's legion
The wolves morphed into ravens, knelt
Praising the crow demon

Manteo sprang with his faithful band
Leapt- save his longhouse haven.
Swept aside like a six years child
By the veiled vengeful raven

His tribe cried out from his building
In the longhouse they'd tried to defend
Grieved they the needless killing

Of Manteo – Of England's friend

Flames licked the towns extinction-
Flambeaux to the longhouse tossed.
To mime Christ's crucifixion
Severed heads were set in a cross

And the witch that bade the warning
Only she they did not see
Only she left alive in the morning
Transformed to a hackberry tree…

9 Days Walk North…

Gibbs skills in repoussage saved them,
Though surviving a forlorn slave.
Still a blacksmiths trade in a coppice
Surpassed being food in a cave

Twas the maid Jane Jones' idea
Urged them to snatch flight chance
For after It finished with her fissure
Blue beast inert in a trance

Jane chancing the Chowan river

With him and a further five
Was the reason the six considered
The six sensed they still alive

Likewise Jane plainly a whopper
Hence wife of Eyanoco.
Six lived to beat his copper
From his mines at Ritanoe

The chief nix a heartless master
Though quick hammering was hard.
And he'd saved them from disaster
But he kept them under guard

Hard work that caused his callouses
To form Eyanoco's art
Was nought to lovelorn fallacies
Beating agonies in his heart

Wounds were her nightly yammering-
Pangs hearing lustful groans…
Her groans got poor John stammering,
As the blacksmith stricken to his bones

Mermerised in the flames of his forge
In wistful melancholy
Torn in the town nestled in the gorge
Thoughts were an injury.
His hurtful thoughts wrought copper
Works. Etched in misery…

Sorrowfully the urns Gibbs made
For his yearnings tempered life
With futile fondness for the maid
That was Eyanoco's wife

Twas on the run that they'd bonded-
It detonated during escape
Though never with love she'd responded
As he comforted her after rape

Love's combustion once ignited
Come dawn that phobic flight
Stayed utterly unrequited
To sear him noon and night

The others had each other.
They'd thanked the Lord for that.

John Wright— Tom Scot hot lovers,
Bob Ellis second son to Pratt

John Gibbs skills as a farrier
Plus Jane's little lady garden
Swung Eyanoco marry her
And grant six more a pardon

Yet his essence sunk in the sewer,
Submerged in self pity.
Though safe 'twas a desolate future
In the hands of the Occaneechi

His guttered soul showed in his craft,
Portrayed in low relief.
Jane's charms set so in copper caste,
Made resplendent by his grief

Though he still feared the bird man
Which featured out of fear
His finest art burst from his heart,
Art fervor a veneer

A veneer that hid his misery

A pretense that cloaked his pain.
Chasing. On her periphery.
Embossing plaques with Jane

The chief expressed delectate-
With his pans and pots and plates.
Bade Gibbs to billet by him
Which emphasized love aches

Twas an atrocious circular
To bunk beside the chief
For as Jane's idol worshipper
Their coitus amassed his grief

And his grief produced such sculpture
In exquisite artifacts
His reward to share their structure-
Loath witness their climax

And Eyanoco hit the mark
Each night to get Her squealing
Whilst John's soul wilted in the dark
-Quenched as the steams of annealing

And Eyanoco quite endowed
And his proud prick much paraded.
Naked, prancing, iron roused
With his testicles both being braided

Roger Pratt oft' stated that
'That Jane Jones always jaded-
Nor nay surprise as a marmot size
In a mouse hole oft' invaded'

Malaise was mirth.
They shamed his worm,
His girth got Pratt's sarcasm.
But it bit hard at night as heard
The howl of her orgasm

Continuously, no flop nor fail
Hear her carnal releases
If failed ignore from his bed of straw
Then he'd pull himself to pieces

The stomach twisting serpent-
Spite summoned to spit bile
'Love'- locked him like a hermit

Till again he'd see her smile
Her smile and hark her murmur
Would snap his solitaire
Allowed him all the firmer
In cloud fantasied affair

Seasons came and seasons went
And the years didn't dent obsession
His metallurgy finest when
He smitten in depression

His works turned most accomplished
And they proved both fine and rare
But bowing to inner conflict
Saw him drowning in despair

And he'd broke all Ten Commandments,
Which enveloped in disgrace
But to sample her enchantments
Hellfire he'd glad embrace

And as a former clergyman
Self loathing wouldn't pass.
A vulgar bygone Puritan

That coveted an ass

John lost in reminiscence
Of fourteen years ago
And of a superior existence
Than slave to Eyanoco

Even when he Matwau's meat
He had a little honour
Not lost, enamored, bade to beat
Hammered pots of copper

Even when he beaten
And headed for Bill's table
He thought her love would sweeten
If protect her he were able

Worse was now. Too humbled.
In that cave he tried protect her.
Too much. The bedstead rumbled
On, as Eyanoco fucked her

And he'd wished he'd been more gallant
And he wished he had more pride

Though dreamt still of her talent
In the cave he wished he'd died

Book 8
Brood of the Brute

Blue Bill Brown-
"Cack candle flicked. Lax life now snatched,
Sea shell with soul vacated.
Doe ye fought n' bit n' scratched
Seething! Still nay placated!"

"What point was she? Fecked factory!
 Mung! Spittin' stillborn sprogs!
Alive a Mam, ift grew mine tree
Nay flayed n' feed for dogs"

"Ift only ye progressed mine line
Do reckon mine blue juices
He'd left ye knot pinned on ye spine,
A Mam may more produces"

"Da Mammas live! Dey canny give
Nurture each mine childs
Ift Mungs be bare what should I's care
Duplex drains n' defiles?"

"Ift nay Mam, den dey Mung-
Nay good for toil or tooling
'N only pleasures when dey young
'Fore dem doo fecked n'spoiling"

"Wee pleasures left do one dis high
Eve' pleadings barely teases!
As teeth sink in another Mung thigh
Delicious pain still pleases!"

"Where can I's go when rules da sky!
All trembles ift I's sneezes!
God emperor! Still wonders I's
Ift dreary doubting eases"

"Dis dreary doubt so weighs mine soul,
Do other Gods so suffer?
Are dey more tight with tithe n' toll?
Shall I's turn ten times tougher?

"Mine flock dis mice, wank wives is lice

Scritch scratch n' ruin n' shame.
When only kin feels what's within
-What courses in dese veins"

"Only brood would feel mine mood-
N' sense mine inner trauma.
'Dis but mine breed knows what's I's need
Dey nears n' I's glows warmer"

"Dis only dem halts much mayhem
With not 'em -nay alone!
Mine kin sweet sing 'Love do my King!'
Dey changed dis cave do home"

"Dis caves a home,
Da first I's known.
Dis dem dat's carved dis mark.
Nowadays seams I's coloured dreams
Before dem dreams w'dark"

"Dey helps do halt dat hellish sound
What whispers, shouts n' titters
What makes I's lost. Dey find I's found
Small saviours. Dem mine critters "

"Dat voice minds I's o' painful finks-

Blessed Mamma, in dat past
Memories oon dat ship o' stinks
When lashed I's on da mast"

"O' bastard Howe – oo'd nay respect
Oo beat mine back more blue.
With Willie Beard, a shaved n' fecked-
Him hacked him gloopy goo"

"Him rose do fight with mighty might
N' smite-ing ones dat flippant
Full grown men a' trembled when
Dey saw da heartbeat quickened"

"Full grown men with pissin' knicks
When He up rose, emerged…
Bears o'men, click cluckin' chicks
When made da anger surge"

"Dose settlers wrong religion fecks
Prayer fooled dem optimistic.
Snick snubbed sweet life o' hurtful sex
It made dem masochistic"

"Prayer turned 'em dry like dat scorched sky
Dat withered all dere crops.

Ift worshipped I's, all've survived
With blood, nay water drops."

"I's laughed der pointless grafting-
Hid under yucca plants
Dat abattoir dey a' crafting
-Dose suck-arse sycophants"

"I's flew at night right o'er them.
Flew -like I's grew'd wings
Remembering der mockings when
I's weak against such fings."

"I's flew n' watched dem reaping
Shit shite dat all dem sowed-
Wuss weeping when dem sleeping-
Flapped flew with dem mine crows"

"I's soared da night oo one o' dem
Da sky do spy our foe
Crows cawed I's a kindred zen
As spied da world below"

"Ift only den dey later knew.
Ift fort took I's as der idol
He wadnay have do all dem slew-

Kirk cranked dem suicidal"

"Dis breathin' God dey shoulda turned
Nay worshipped dat dead Jesus!
'Doo late! Doo late! Doo late we learned!
Da living Matwau sees us!"

Matwau-
"Kill dat cunt! He craves do die!
Low life a canny lettie linger
For staring us – straight eye do eye-
Sight eyes be rings for fingers"

Blue Bill Brown-
"What dis da voice screams in mine head?
Dat sears I's into riot.
A fargone Father long since dead
Dat ceases do be quiet?"

"Gruff growl dis loud, drowning mine
It frets I's into fits!
Dis demonic 'gainst mine divine-
Sly arguments persists"

"I's beats mine head do beat away
Grey ghoul dat guides mine choices
Brow beats I's bloody dat pray may

Silence vexatious voices"

Matwau-
"Another bitch we'll hold do fire,
Watch cook n' cock increases!
A brizzle burn for oor desire
Cums consider Mung life ceases"

Blue Bill Brown-
"Which devil a' witch do blame dis glitch?
Jib jabbers drives I's mental!
Provokes I's more do act more raw
Possessed mine inner temple"

"Dis mine children stops dat din
Dey laughs- He shushin' silent.
So steeped in sin dis inner djinn.
In sleeps He seeps in violence"

"Mamma! So sorely pined!
He comes ye memory fades
True try rehearse old words o' kind
Do conquer His tirades".

 "Finks of Mam plus mine blue brood
Plus praise from slaves n' sages-

Fulfilled with food may calms mad mood-
Nay lewd with red hot rages"

Matwau-
"Carve cunts dat left inferior gifts
Make suffer frugal folly!
Throw dat tight tribe oft dem cliffs
Do fill us both with jolly"

Blue Bill Brown-
"Or try sit content when life dis sweet
N'want do coolin' calm
His torments I's do tear more meat,
Do serve more Mungs more harm"

"I's feel do weep but den mine tears
Quish quench da burning sun
A splash oon flabbergasted ears
Den all respect be done"

"Den out da darkened blackened planet
 Somefing worse would take mine helm
Somefing cold n' hard as granite
Well worse dan I's would rule dis realm"

"Know I's is cruel n' I's perverse

Still vital do suppress
For He who dwells within I's worse
Rip wreck dis whole Mung mess"

"Titch Agnes who be Mammas spit
Seems most do make Him run
Seems wheelin' steer from frenzied fit
She is mine golden one"

"She be captain dis mine ship,
Mine other brood be crew
Da brood be in apprenticeship
Do steer dis vessel through"

"Rip rack Him oot mine mangled mind
Ift seek He dem corrupt
Mine self I's deaf n'dumb n' blind
Ift He would interrupt"

Matwau-
"Dey'll kill us ift dey get dat chance
Know dis! N' be prepared
Slay a son much in advance-
Compliance ift dem scared"

Blue Bill Brown-
"O' cack caked curse dat gets Him riled-

Seamen with pallid skin…
Sour Mung Euro-pricks reviled
Dey wakes mine inner twin"

"Bread buffoons dat come explore
Like reeky coral ghosts.
Who seek mine gold inside Mine shore-
Thieves in dem creeky boats!"

"Em pasty folk would feck invoke
Red rage till last oon slaughter.
A capricious save from tortured grave-
Salt slut, da governors daughter."

"Oh she will live, for almost fam'
Though sickened by her sight
For now, as faved Agnes' Mam
Pink slag have earned dat right"

"But try escape she one more time
N' I's will lets Him ride…
Try she n' for treason crime-
Splash splish her pink insides"

Matwau
"Grasp yo girls.. Grrrowing fast!

Into succuless-sense
How much longer can Us last
Do taste exquisite essence?"

Blue Bill Brown-
"Why don't dey gaze with eyes amours?
Why bitches keep love hidden?
Don't I's supply slags with succour?
Dey show no lust when ridden'!"

"Why eyes not sparkle with jump joy?
Like eyes alight mine litter.
Why Mung crumble cold n' coy
When gifted up dem shitter?"

"When Godly gift dem shitty shaft
Why don't dem Mungers faun?
 Dis I's not den a master crafts-
God at poopen porn?"

Matwau-
"We craves a toy- go grab a boy!
Caress us with sob cries
We needs do play on dis dull day
Quit quiet when Mung dies!"

Blue Bill Brown-
"Dere it dis, mine moon again

Glow calls oon I's do conquer
Bright beams seem break His bondage chain
Nighttime's dis signs I'll prosper"

"Nighttime dis time o' plans be made
Plush plans do own whole world!
Da plan do every patch invade
For frail false gods be purged"

"De plans do own each tree, each stone
N'exorcise dis twin
Do conquer all the earth alone
N' conquer Him within"

Matwau-
"We are da dark. All men's deep fear
Da fright dat men not knows
We dis da whisperings men hear -
We are dere shadow foes"

"We dis da Lord o' bitey beasts-
Night beasts mine loyal whores.
We blessed by squarks o' vampire bats
N' squeaks o'rats -but more dan dat-
By crows with royal caws"

"We dis da fing dat men must keep
Buried in dere dungeons
Da nightmare creep dat makes dem weep-

A Father o' Melungeouns"

"Look in dat fire- hear dragons speak
N' tell o' Our vocation
Do spread from oot da Chesapeake
Do colonize dis new nation'

"Turn red skin a purple shade
Da brown a grayer hue
Da pinks more do a lilac grade.
Refine da blood with blue"

"Get feckless more- more copulate
Feck more- f'righteous fight
Oot breed for do oot populate
Do rob da retching whites."

"Da retchy whites dat will def come
N' claim dese sacred places
Swarming oot dere fetid slums-
Infectious pale faces"

"Cum- go a feckin', killin'
Spare scant da mercy's hand
For yesterweeks peak villain will
Be Lord o' all da land"

Narrator-
The tranquil captive audience
Only galvanized his rave
-Inflamed a wrathful radiance

To irradiate the cave

Cringing slaves sat calcified
Which turned his rantings worse.
And traversing echos amplified
Twin tortures of the curse

Blue Bill Brown-
"O'er da rippling ears o'corn
Swayin' in da sun cast morn
O'er da dappled shadowed ground
A mischief comes do take I's crown"

"Dey forgin' forth in feline prowl
Disguised dey is in cloakin' cowl
Pretendin' still do worship I's
Rebellion thus dis in disguise"

"Dey wish de-throne I's off mine seat
Dose pretend devout
Dose fake lick mine arse n' feet
Glissade for royal rout"

"I's hears dem when I's lay do rest
I's see dem whence I's drowse
Cuckoos claiming dis mine nest-

Urge Him go forth de-louse"

"Make I's release mine deputy
Crush dem dat fink dey rival
Summon mine mortal enemy
For mine own survival"

"Da looks dey look when looks mine way!
I's knows dey itch do take…
All dat praise dat dey all say
Now knows dis feckin' fake"

 "Dey'll get I's when I's dis asleep
-No man can take I's woke!
Dey fink dem wolf- dem feckin' sheep
Sheep o' de Roanoke!"

Matwau-
"And yet ye call Me enemy!
Gemini o' Bill de Brown
But who steps up do defend We?
Do safeguard dis oor crown!"

"Who indeedy fecks oor foe?
Dis it de softer double?
Or perhap' dis be da harder bro
Dat gets we oot o' trouble"

"Ye castigates all de kills
-Mammas treacle traitor!
Castigates but always will-
Always glad I ate her"

"Always glad dat I's doon here,
When Bill boy might surrender
When Billy Brown a doon with fear
Steps Matwau! Oor defender!"

"Dis I's controls da crows n' fings
Dat guides oor hands do kill…
Dat lets us soar as if with wings
Nay Mamma's pussy Bill!"

"Snot Mammas sucklin'goody guy!
-Same guy she nay did want!
Shame ye harsh oon ye ally-
Finks Matwau dis a cunt!"

"Dis cunt dat dwells de darker place-
Dat place ye scared do goes.
Dat hell dat ye well will embrace
Do vanquish-ed oor foes"

"Dat hellish pit dat saves ye skin
When danger dis a brewin'
Den Matwau springs, oor tougher twin
With cunts cravin' a subduing!"

Blue Bill Brown-
"Da Dom! Da hate! Da Dom! Da howl!

Da fings He finks are fings most foul!
Da Dom! Da Damned His foulness be
Dat foulness dat drains into me!"

"Damned be dat bangin' in mine ears!
Endured dat drum for years n' years!
N' years! With fingers deep in ears
Do try do muffle thrumpin' thrum!
What thrums mine dome n'makes I's numb!"

Matwau-
"Now time do stop ye whimperin'-
Time I's took da reigns
Else You- Bill- be a fritterin'
Da grip on oor domains"

"N' feck da brood, dey future food
Ift would we eat dem last
A gamble bet, def' doon fat neck
Dey'd go ift 'nother fast"

"Ye canny see, ift doon do thee
'Twood End in a disaster
Back ye down now bruvver Brown
Do maintain Matwau master"

"Fecked ye chance with brood in trance-
Time do close dat portal...
An age o'cruel with One us rule-
I's...Matwau – De immortal!"

Book 9
Wahunsonacock

December 1607. Virginia.

Narrator-
Jamestown camp lay ravaged,
Frozen, running out of food.
Ransacking's by the savages
Cast a bitter crushing mood.

Its leaders ordered Smith explore,
To seek out native allies.
To trade or raid to top towns store
Before the townships demise.

In a vast and frosty wasteland
Up the Chickahominy
Smith surrounded by a war band
Of two hundred Pamunkey.

Yanked out of an icy marsh,
Marched miles of barren plateaux.

Through woods, wide streams and head high
grass
To Werowocomoco.

Throughout the town Smith dragged around
With whoops of gloat and glory.
To the longhouse, bound, to sit astounded
By the sovereigns story.

Chief Powhatan-
"Captain Smith, I'll tell you if
Protect you Pocohontos.
For It was one. Would others come
Disaster be upon us."

"My daughter saved your pale neck.
Suspect so for good reason.
So go retell my saga back.
I confide in your liaison."

"So harken!
For with tell this, I've saved the life of you
For you back to tell all Jamestown
The things I had to do…"

"It bought the woe to Roanoke

To taint tribes of us naked.
Bought disease, disgust, despair,
Convinced us It was sacred."

"I'd never ever seen Its like
Like Its corrupted sin,
Like feasting on the flesh of men
Or laying with your kin."

"Like mating with the dying,
Then used the fucked for broth.
Drank tears the doomed were crying
To fuel ferocious wroth."

"It bore down to the under
To release demons of greed
Who flocked the flame haired thunder
To share Its man flesh feed."

"It Atasaya incarnate.
Was uglier than Okee.
It murdered, mauled and maimed and ate
The Potomac to Pamunkey."

"It turned that anglophilic chief
To despise your little isle.

Replaced his faith with disbelief
His loyalty with bile."

"It stoked a bilious hatred.
Bile caused Wanchese to croak.
With the chieftainship vacated
It ruled the Roanoke."

"It ruled them and It schooled them
When It drained them of their force.
Its maxim was in mayhem as
It steered them all off course."

"It distorted deity spirits.
It sickened weak men's souls.
It pressed me to my limits
By pushing forth Its goals."

"Now you may say I'm savage
For I dealt a heavy hand.
But you white hands came to ravage
When you landed in my land."

"At first you made me to believe
That you came here to trade.
It's in your marrow to deceive,

To rob, to wreck, to raid."

"You came, you burnt and then you learnt
You needed us to nourish!
You stole our corn, after you warned-
Malice not to flourish."

"It's in your marrow, yet I see
All men can act as swine!
Far crueler is the one that He
Believes that He divine"

"Far crueler Its fanatics!
The kind that It subverted.
The sane veered to erratics
By the word of the perverted."

"This inhumane behavior,
Appalling acts so odd
Was sanctioned by a 'saviour'.
It saw Itself a God"

"Crow God-'Okee'. Fickle. Fake
Crafty, cruel and clever.
An outer state like burnished plate.
Inside was black crow feather."

"The Mohammedans, them ochre skinned
Left a year 'fore they
I scattered to a fairer wind
And Still they thrive today."

"We met! I saw it in their desperate eyes
That they were wronged, deceived.
Abandoned by your English lies...
 I granted their reprieve."

"So men can stay and share this land
And live a life of bliss.
If men give more than they demand.
If men take not the piss."

"If men will live in harmony
Then I will let men live!
If spread they not perversity
Forebears nay not forgive."

"Matwau came and just Its name
As purgatory night!
Its deeds of shame spread swift like flame
To set our world alight."

"It came, campaigned. From Engerland
And sought sanctification.
It claimed This was Its holy land.
Hallowed by Its invasion."

"No bear, no wolf, no wolverine
Was Matwau's fury rival.
Migrates with Its mujahideen
Caused carnage on arrival."

"Yet such butchery went so unspoke
For more than fourteen summers.
A blanket bowdlerizing cloak
Was cast to gag all utters"

"Rumours, whispers, tokens,
Finds of carcasses torn bloody.
Some tried to read the omens,
Some blamed the Pukwudgie."

"Nuttah! My heart!
Too soon, at twelve for she depart,
When life for her had barely start.
Taken by Its nightmares knife!
Sad still for second favorite wife!"

"Missing from the meadow
Sent to the afterlife,
I'll rejoin she as a shadow
Now vanquish-ed this strife."

"I informed soon of this issue
When found she in lagoon.
She stripped of every sinew.
Eye sockets stuffed with plumes."

"I overflowed with vengefulness
To cleave the guilty head.
I demanded gathered evidence
As Nuttah neat in bed."

"Twas only strict commanding
That more cases came to know.
Witnesses expanding
Past ordeals with feathered foe."

"All my priests then prophesied
That cunt that came crusade.
Foresaw the one that qualified,
The one that they portrayed."

"They'd read some signs in entrails.

Read eagles in their flight,
Had proved with clued credentials
The cause of all this blight."

"Foresaw potential triumph
As It bred and spread Its seed.
It'd busted scores of hymens
To champion Its creed."

"My sorcerers saw symptoms
As they read the stormy skies,
Foresaw barbaric kingdoms
From the seeds of emerald eyes."

"Foretold that no mere normal man
To best It would enough.
Concocted spells seek he who can-
Found Opechancanough!"

"So gathered us all the gallant
From the thirty tribes of mine.
The braves with combat talent
Ordered track down the malign."

"Aft' many moons my mavens,
And counsellors of war

Diagnosed the rot was ravens,
And in order to restore
Must purge from all locations
 Matwau's scope to spore."

"Dear brother with four hundred
For nearly four full years
Sought out and tortured, hunted-
The copper crow adheres.

"I did not seek negotiate
To reveal kept secret layers.
I found by modes excruciate
The cave of Atasaya."

"We hurted Its devotees
Who'd like a plague had spread
Its broadening diocese,
Enlarged Its range of dread."

"Smoke, Smith, my pipe of peace.
Now wash your hands in water.
Relax, recline, eat of this feast-
Hear why I gave no quarter."

"A werowance called Parahunt,

In scout for russet flock
Stumbled on a reverent,
A chief of Chowanoc."

"His spotter in a hop-hornbeam
Had told of seeing things-
This chief by a secluded stream
Had signed the folded wings."

"Parahunt with ninety
Attacked the caravan!
The fight they fought was mighty
And they slaughtered to a man."

"The Chowanoc's fought to final breath
Whilst sounding cawing sounds,
As if they sought a caustic death.
As if Elysium bound."

"Not one did to surrender-
Those followers of the wing.
As slayed sang they the splendour
Of their tawny cannibal King."

"Still more reports come filtering
Of doctrine spread around.

An orthodoxy simmering
In a Tuscarora town."

"Opechancanough, my chief, the bear
With forty mounted horses
In seeking finding Matwau's lair
Pillaged with his forces"

"It was a blazing blood soaked dusk,
Felled families of fanatics.
They tore the town to smoldered husk
To purge of foul dogmatics."

"The town head man was forced confess,
That chief of Ocanhonan.
To tell from were the tendrils spread-
Shot dead by forty bowmen."

"Gave Opechancanough a lead
Up Powhatan river
He paddled miles in manic speed
For justice to deliver."

"A snaking convoy of canoes
Went west to seek man-eater.
The wicked one was now pursued,

Loomed time for grim dictator."

"Thirty strains and thirty rests,
Troops tired, at end of tether.
Some faltered in this righteous quest
-Talk was It ruled the weather."

"The thunder rolled, the rain it lashed
Till half the paddle boats be smashed.
His war band ran on feet four days
Disorientated by the haze"

"The forest lost to mist!
The wind to fearsome blow.
My brother forced insist
The men proceed to go"

"At night in huddled clusters,
Fearful of feared foe!
Wind whipped sound boomed blusters,
That howled at 'em to go."

"He beat and screamed the men proceed,
They frigid, full of fright.
For it seemed the trees did bleed
In this realm of night."

"Bleeding trees bore people fruit
Which clattered from bare branches.
As neared the village of the brute,
Smacked by savage avalanches."

"His blitz surprise was nullified
By screaming sentinels.
The soldiery stood stultified
By crowing decibels."

"Crows darked the skies and with their cries
Darked my armies daring.
The crying caws tipped men and squaws
To charge in ready, raring."

"They dropped from trees, out under leaves
Behind, before, about!
Surrounded big Powhatan chief
And sought to check him out."

"They circled as they growled and snarled,
Those of the aberration.
Those black souls a twisted, gnarled-
Filtered down each generation."

"Shaven scalps on savage louts
Attacked us with steel hatchets.
Giant men or beasts we ken
The bandits were about us!"

"Toothless crones likes bags of bones,
Lime eyed infants lobbing stones
Squaws on fours were chanting verses
Men fat on man fat spat curses."

"My kin snatched crows from out of air
That tried peck out his eyes.
Saw to those encircled there
A much distressed demise."

"His solid stance magnificence -
Men countered in attack.
All perished pained, all in a trance
The possessed Pocoughtronack."

"A genocide! He skinned alive
Each man, each squaw, each leaching child.
He shot and stomped, their dogs got kicked-
ed
This town of the damned wing addicted.
Killed them all those crow convicted.

Killed to stop what was predicted".

"He wiped Its base. Now he in race
To slay It in Its nest
For learned of It, blue skin in fire hair face,
Tenacious in our quest"

"Night and day and through two moons,
Smashed with gale 'pon gale.
In battered rain, blind by monsoon
But still he did not fail."

"Now listen Smith and listen well
The closure of this tune
It raised it up, your Christian Hell
And formed it in the dunes."

"The beach was black. Awash with crows
And tied in rows and rows and rows
The old, the young, the bare, the clothed
Shrieking screams of wasted woes."

"The woe was soup that thicked the air
None could breathe from their despair.
All shivered in the long grass there
Too numb to move, but morbid stare!"

"Prostrate under flags of skin
Glazed watched a ritual begin
They buzzed and stung as devil bees
Demented in dance ceremonies!"

"They danced, in chant,
They touched, they torched
Till all that we could smell was scorched
Flesh, and all that we could only hear
Was yells and whoops and woeful fear!"

"A hundred men! But we had more!
Dim watched more horror shows in store.
Then saw them turn to kneel and wave
Toward cruel cliffs, toward hells cave!"

"There! There flame and ice in one foul face
As thunder bit the beach
Lightning strikes struck heads on pikes
As paced It whilst It preached!"

"Arrows flew! After flew flight
Streamed down the dunes onto the fight-
As if the day attacked the night
Their souls burnt black as our souls white

We mighty with the law!"

"War! War!' A thousand caws!
Its crows caused our bones rattle
Crows urged the fight on this dread night
Us and those brutes to battle"

"Us flock seagulls flew to the fray
Attacked the vicious crows
'Twas grey carnage in that bay,
For our dark souled foes"

"Kin who hath a soul of white
Smote scores of charcoal swine
My warlord slayer soon spied Atasaya
Up killer crags he climbed"

"The demon in delirious dream
Sneered down his scaling duel
And pissed a steaming arc-ed stream
To throw the fight more fuel"

Matwau-
"Comes challenge We, ye sly gentile?
Despoiler of mine land!
Up! For judgement waits by trail

By dese theistic hands."

"Ye pagan dog o' lesser Gods
Weak fool! You'll beg submission!
Dare'st come! Thy will succumb
Mine holy inquisition!"

"We speaketh as da one true Lord
-Da maker o' da mists!
See! -We casts aside mine sword
Do sentence death from fists!"

Opechancanough-
"Silence snake! Son of blue moon!
Killer without good reason.
Prepare atone for The Ahone
Shal'st cure of ye strewn poison."

"Poisons spread from where you tread-
Drained from thy azure veins
I shall reclaim from toxins lain
Poor slaves free of thy chains"

Matwau-
"Dare defy a lion!- Dog!
A duck oo dares a hawk!

We'll spike thy head upon mine rod-
Minch munch upon thy stalk"

"We'll prop thine eyes do see thy woe-
See We devouring thee.
Thy minions dat stare oop below
Bow beg on bended knee!"

Opechancanough-
"Cannibal! Okee's beast!
Eater of men's essence!
Breathe thy last thy dark realm priest
'For death brings obsolescence!"

Chief Powhatan-
"The cymbal clash of the behemoths!
My brother rained It blows
Hope vape, vanquish the regime of
This fiend fermenting woe."

"It took punch hits of Opechank.
Took till kin to knees had sank.
Then roared Its devils triumph roar
-It beat down brother flat to floor."

"Abukcheech, my chief, with thirteen braves,

Felled as they rushed It in waves.
It split their skulls with tomahawks
To build a barricade of corpse.
A barrier blocking off Its cave.
Sealed in Opechancanough
Time 'nough now to finish off."

"As little brother lost life's will
As Matwau went in for cold kill
As Matwau crazed with raw raised axe
It stopped and shuddered, staggered back!"

"Its eyes went glazed as gripped in dream.
Behind a woman's winning scream.
From Its mouth spout black blood flying
It swung Its axe and She fell dying."

"As It swayed with quizic frown
Op'chank fumbled, found
A fallen spear, with which Kin heft
Through the injured ogres chest."

"Then again, then heft some more
Till wallowed deep in demon gore.
In and out spear weapon working.
Matwau simply stood there smirking."

"It smirked as if it all a joke.
Smirked until the spear broke.
They two stood still in silent stare.
Stood in silence in Its lair."

"An age was stood as if time stopped.
Its rage was passed, and then It dropped.
My brother prod. Test It dead.
Cursed It. Kicked and then beheaded."

"'Lord! Lord!' Its crow crew cried
As they crowd inside
And clocked their murdered King.
Crows collapsed, croaked, died
Whence spied Its demise-
"Twas strange and curious thing."

"When cut through the gruesome hack,
When Matwau's head was put in sack
A snivel heard from the pitch black
And pushing back the black crow stack
To inspect he circled back."

"He paused to pick the ragged crone,
As life drained from her sagging bones

And with a rag he wiped 'way grime,
Saw elegance there of once her prime."

"Saw beneath the dirt, decay
A loveliness seemed sculpt of clay.
In fade but beauty still there rife.
This beauty who had saved his life"

Opechancanough-
"Who art thee that save-ed me
And why is my heart rent?
And why my tears and have my prayers
Been hailed - art spirit sent?"

"Why did I not find before?
Why now in death we meet?
Thy purity outshines this gore
-Dilute this grim thy sweet"

"Thy suffered well in this sour hell
Now suffer no more fear
Though now I tell with heart in swell-
Run free ye phantom deer!"

Chief Powhatan-
"For stood by his side there stood a doe

Which glowed with fur of radiant snow.
It nuzzled him once then turned to go.
Her spirit flew now freed from woe"

"His life was saved, he dug her grave.
My brother struck, beguiled.
From that cave a debt repaid,
He saved her sobbing child."

"He saved that child then married her,
She bears his children, three.
Though Matwau's blood sons do transfer
We are as family."

"Her sons will rule some tribes one day-
Three chiefs through mothers line.
But schooled they in ancestral ways.
Part red - but trice benign."

"A gift was took. A gift I'll give-
I offer Amonute, a daughter.
May chance our two tribes would forgive
And steer from senseless slaughter."

"Cast ye gaze blue Matwau's head,
At this unholy vision!

See for yourself who'd spread the dread-
Of dread forged fake religion."

Epilogue

January 5th 1617. Palace of Westminster.
London, England.

Narrator-
The Royal sphincter, saggy and spent,
Twelfth more years of pounding,
Was dangerously discontent.
John Rolfe was there recounting.

Rolfe's hardy baccy botany
Had saved the Jamestown flop.
Now leader of that colony-
Made rich with baccy crop.

Rolfe wed Powhatan's daughter.
They'd invite Westminster palace
Where spoke of essential slaughter

Of the second Sawney malice.

The King cringed tell of Matwau's hell
Conscious of Matoaka
-The princess gagging on the smell
Seeping out his cracker.

James sat in shit in fluster.
Thought to figure who the fault.
Blamed the colonies investor -
The secular sir Walt.

Raleigh, skating on thin ice
For spurning gay approaches
Was soon to pay a heady price
For subjects Rolfe was broaching.

America, and Raleigh's theme
To raise the English flag.
Damned him to die for dare to dream,
Thoughts suckled on a fag.

The atheist antagonized,
No sign of El Dorado!
No gold or parting of the thighs,
Rebuffed Him with bravado.

And now in foreign places
There were seeds of James' shame.
Same seed that caused more faeces.
Bean seed with native names.

Pocohontos got so gravely ill-
James vowed aloud vendettas
Swore in shout his banes to kill-
Promised plague his debtors.

Swore he'd neutralize all offspring
Vowed he'd use all of his means
Hunt all kin born to the wing-
Exterminate the Beans.

Lord Enn sat in attendance
Knew the fallout from this scene
Knew ordered duel the menace -
Slay the seeds of Sawney Bean.

Rebecca Rolfe set home to sail
Leaving James to fester-
Nay noble King more like a frail
Foul and sour court jester.

Poor Pocahontas died that spring-
The virus hard to weather.
Caught her ailment off of the King,
Who raved the tale forever.

Rolfe buried her in a grave in Kent
Then fled cross the Atlantic
Left the King his hatred vent
That saw him foaming frantic.

James just released his holy book
Now blank with degradation
Vowed destroy the tainted look
Of those born in that new nation.

The starving time was at an end-
Opechancanough relented
Relationships were on the mend-
Reversed by He tormented.

King James-
"Reappeared! Dread red hair infernal!
My ears do ring of Rolfe's vocal portal!
Bean again, as if eternal!
As if that fucking red's immortal"

"Oh how my poor ears shrilly ring!
And the ring is getting shriller!
There is no rest for Gods own King
Till end seeds of the cannibal killer"

"It is I by God elected,
It is I who's in the lurch.
I, divined by God anointed
Who must kill to serve the church"

"God made I the divine ruler
Sent to govern by His hand,
Not to tolerate them that crueller-
That son that sailed to that new land"

"Bean tribe still so are painful thorny!
Pricks in me for all it's worth.
Now grandsons of that killer Sawney
Still do pollute my hallowed earth!"

Narrator-
The King ordered royal censors
To wipe most of John Smiths journal,
Forbade, on death, to chatter,
Talk, or write upon this matter
To bury deep the dreadful history

Of the tragic eaten colony.

James paid for agitators
In Tuscarora spies
Financed a red genocide
To wipe the emerald eyes.

Massacred the native tribes
In forests, towns and beaches.
A multitude would lose their lives
Motive of fecal breaches.

Embarrassment by prophesies
Powhatan was proclaiming,
The mess, the myths, the cannibals.
The copied case inflaming.

James flames a stoked what went down there.

King James-
"That fucking flaming ginger hair!
This Chief that killed It in Its lair.
I'm The One! No Powhatan!
Who'd stopped red devil's spread."

Narrator-

…But again he'd pooped his pantalon-
So banned it writ or read.

King James-
"I have on My side angels!
Seems Sawney's seeds the CROws!
I'll expurgate false fables-
Free the world o' fibber foes!"

"Could it be this blasphemy o'
   Roanoke's woeful plight-
   Omens fulfilled with thousands killed-
   Another Sawney blight?
   Things bride Anne said as tearful bled-
   Oh! Most regret I scorning-
   Anne the vile's most infantile
   Noisy wedding warning"

King James 1st and Sawney's genes
Marked next the foul relations -
Initiated war machines
In Powhatan-Anglo nations.

They'd contaminated the new world-
Friends transformed to fiends.

Virginia's holocaust unfurled
By James Stuart and the Beans.

Matwau was not the last one-
Madman believed messiah.
More rejects were to follow on
As sheep will seek pariahs.

The End.

Mat Horton-
A Short Life

My family- Horton- hailed from the Black
Country, England. From Dudley to be precise.
Originally this branch of the Horton line worked
in agriculture in Yorkshire, later migrating south
following industry in the early 19th century. For
generations the Hortons worked at first in the
coal mines and then in the grim steel factories
and mills that had sprung up all over the

industrial West Midlands.'Black by day, Red by night' was the saying.

 These factories powered the industrial revolution, supplying the British empire with tools, weapons and machinery.

It was from this hard, grimy semi-slavery slum like conditions that my father John, upped, aged 30, and escaped.

Handsome and ambitious, John travelled to London with my teenage mother Jennifer and after working as a model maker on Stanley Kubricks '2001' applied for a job at the BBC in 1967.

It was the beginning of the golden age of British television. Through unrestrained enthusiasm for this new found magic and ridiculous hours put in on his own back (up to 20 a day, 6 or 7 days a week) he quickly rose to SFX Designer, working on all the classics like Monty Python, The Goodies, Dad's Army, Are You Being Served?, It Ain't Half Hot Mum, Some Mother's Do Ave Em, Dr. Who, Rentaghost etc.

A highlight that I can still remember when I was very young was working on Monty Python and the Holy Grail in Scotland. My sister and I had small parts as extras in the wedding and 'bring out yer dead' scenes and John as well as doing the SFX explosions and rigs – including delimbing the Black Knight (played in part by Richard Burton or John Silver as my father called him who was a double amputee. He had lost both his legs in the battle of Arnhem) and the killer rabbit- was cast as one of french taunters. He was the knight at the bottom of the crenellations throwing 'wanker' signs.

Our house was somewhat unique, which offended and upset the net curtain twitching beige neighbours into frequent and embarrassing public shouty fits.

A twenty foot polystyrene boot from the 'Spike Milligan show -Q(10?)' filled the front garden attracting noisy delinquent kids from the surrounding area to play on and swing on the boot laces. The bean stalk from 'Goodies and the Beanstalk' threaded its way up the outside of the house. The Tardis sat to one side of the front garden, surrounded by a dozen rusting cars.

It was like a museum.

That quiet orderly cul de sac echoed with the honk of geese, the barking and braying of dogs and horses and the revs of numerous small motorcycles. The vanilla street was further flavoured with the yells and rattle and pop of air guns as us feral kids shot at each other. The still suburban air was split with screams when someone fell off the death slide. Inside were entire rooms festooned with severed heads, legs and arms from the cult classic 'Deathline', spaceships and monsters from Dr, Who and empty cider bottles pathetically hidden by my mother.

Whilst John had clawed his way out of working class into middle class and was now living the dream, working on challenging and interesting shows, sleeping with creative colleagues, sometimes the dancers on 'Top of the Pops' and mixing with some of the brightest, funniest and funkiest people in Britain at that time, Jenny bought her inner council slum with her to our 'posh' (more like 'Steptoe's yard. The hoarding of clutter is something that I am affected with and I have to be very strict with myself to throw things away) home in Windsor.

Whilst my fathers family were proud- if poor- working class (my grandfather Frank, unusually for that time and place, was a great lover of books and of Victorian adventurers and dreamt of becoming a writer himself) Jenny's family were what we'd call now call the sub class. Chavs.

Her mother, Minnie was rumored to prostitute herself – for drink money- and would abandon her three hungry kids to wander the streets alone all night long. Her first husband committed suicide and killed their first child in tragic unexplained circumstances. Minnie was violent and would smash her little council house up in drunken rages and slash the clothes of her second husband, my grandfather Jack, with an open razor. Minnie would often call Jack a simpleton in public. She always reminded me of Bette Davis in 'Whatever Happened to Baby Jane'.

That drink addled demon reappeared in Minnie's youngest child Jennifer – my deranged Mother. Outwardly it was an enviable childhood.

My friends would often tell me I was spoilt. I would have happily given away that bizarre life and all my expensive toys for a stable home. Almost every night of the week I'd lay awake listening to the screams and swearing and breaking of glass and smashed furniture of Jenny's terrifying drink soaked tantrums. Every morning they'd be blood stained devastation. Her voice would change and deepen after a bottle of cheap cider and I still shudder to remember her growling slurring obscenities when she'd utter all manner of foul lies and nonsense and threats.

I saw 'The Exorcist' at twelve and whilst my friends were frightened out of their wits I remember thinking this is what my mother is like most nights.

My father worked away a lot on location and although this halted the explosive arguments, my sister Emma and I would be twice as nervous as we were without our protector and Jenny was utterly unstable and unpredictable on cider.

I was the teeny tiniest pupil in my whole school, and not very bright which in the 1970's was a recipe for humiliation and bullying.

I was useless at school partly because I was exhausted. When John was home there was fighting in the night, often with the police being called, and when he was away Jenny would get twice as sloshed and fall asleep in front of the television. At midnight the 'off' transmission whine as Television ceased broadcasting woke me up constantly. I would have to get out of bed and tread down those dark scarey stairs to reach over my comatose mother to switch all the lights and the white noise off.

Jenny would often put on an upperclass voice in public and tell everyone that she lived on top of St.Leonards Hill, an exclusive part of royal Windsor and that her husband was in the film industry. People thought her a terrible snob. In reality she was always firmly rooted in the filth and chaos and the squalor of her council owned rough nick estate in Dudley.

I was scared of her.
But Emma has it worse. My mother hated her.
As Emma matured the hatred grew and they
would fist fight and Jenny would say the most
appalling things to her own daughter.
I learned to be conciliatory and to tread carefully
around the alcoholic madwoman but Emma
never gave an inch and it hardened her.
-Emma pulled herself through this traumatic
period the best of all of us. She now has a lovely
family of her own and is well regarded and
respected in the film industry.
As I entered my teenage years severe acne hit
hard to further rock my fragile confidence. In
amidst of this catastrophic war zone my hopeless
parents decided to have another child…?
And things inevitably got worse. I did not have
a mother's love. I was short, spotty and thick
and so dating girls was always disastrous with
my lack of confidence. I did have a good sense
of humour thanks to endless hours listening to
Python records and my humorous eccentric
father and I would boast that I could tell a joke
on any subject. I could hold my own in a fight,
on account of me being pushed around all the
time by the relentless bullies..
I spent most of my teenage time out on the
streets, up to no good, as home life was so

diabolical. John had taken to tapping the phone as Jenny had started to make credible death threats. He found out that she was delving into witchcraft and had tried to hire a hitman to bump him off. The police were informed. He used to tell me all the sordid details on excruciatingly long nights. I thought it was therapy for him to talk on and on, little realizing the damage it was doing to myself by hearing these things. Parents should not tell their children of their grubby secrets.

He also knew, thanks to the bug, of all the teenagey things Emma and I got up with our respective friends – and told me what he knew- something for which I'll never forgive him.

And then one sunny day Jenny simply left. She'd met this fat slimy wicked little fellow drinker. She left on her own but after realizing or more likely being told she came back and took Amelia, my four year old sister with her. It was her meal ticket to the house.

John had a complete mental breakdown, gave up work and spent most of his time in bed or shuffling around aimlessly on all fours in his underpants rambling on and on about the mistakes he had made in his life.

Jenny, who was always very sociable, and on the guidance and advise of her new boyfriend used

Amelia as a weapon to get possession of the house by accusing John of sexual abuse of his own daughter.

He was not charged through lack of evidence as Emma and I were always around during the limited access visits as a precautionary measure- as we both knew how her twisted mind worked- but the social services believed her – she could put on a good show mid morning before the alcohol kicked in- and so all access visits were ceased. Jenny told everyone who leant her half an ear the devious and evil lies that she had installed in Amelia before she moved away from the area and so we became pariahs, distrusted by friends and neighbors.

John spent almost all of his fortune on an unwinable custody battle.

We lost our large home in the divorce settlement and I went off traveling Europe.

After all that unforgivable evilness I learned that Jenny later turned catholic and had Amelia baptized. So that was all right then. Her black soul was saved.

Ten years later - after Jenny had squandered all of her much larger share of the settlement and only then had pathetically died when she fell drunkenly down the stairs (pushed by her murderous boyfriend my father believes) and

Amelia had come to live with me in my new house – (John had become a bum, a shabby hobo living rough in a caravan on a field, tending a herd of goats and looking like one)- I asked her why, aged four, did she tell those horrible stories, that I knew were not true, to the police and social services. She told me that Jenny had told her that she would die if she did not repeat it. That she would fall down dead if she did not absolutely repeat word for word this sordid story, a story that must have taken the horrible couple weeks to concoct and further weeks to make a toddler repeat over and over again. Police and social services did not listen or care or want to know anymore the lives that they had potentially fucked up and Amelia would not press charges against that 'stepdad'. It was abuse still, though nothing physical, and I still believe Paul Allen, my mother's boyfriend, should have been punished for his part in putting dirty stories in a child's head.

As predicted Amelia was and remains fragile, neurotic and damaged. Thanks authorities. A good job…

So, it was not the easiest start in life.

I do consider myself damaged – if self repaired-goods.

One thing that John installed in me before his

fall was an industrial discipline.

He was always creative, practical, active and never lazy and this helped me when I entered the film industry at the tender age of fifteen on that wonderful film 'Labyrinth'.

On the first week of work I saw David Bowie in Elstree studios, I'd an instant unrequited crush with the lead actress Jennifer Connolly, fallen into the bog of eternal stench, stumbled into a goblin house where I witnessed the extraordinary sight of a dwarf orgy and hurled a polystyrene rock so hard that it had wiped out three sword and axe armed goblins from which I copped a bollocking from the Kermit sounding director, Jim Henson, giving me first the frights and then the giggles.

I would work extremely long hours in the film industry and I would love every minute of it. Hard work took my mind away from most of the rotten memories. I have now worked on over fifty movies since then and dozens of tv shows and music videos. Some projects have been terrific – Band Of Brothers and The Pacific , currently 'The Crown' and 'Harlots', Sleepy Hollow, Bond films, 101 Dalmations, where I took home one of the puppies who was my all time best (long deceased) friend Dillon, an amazing animal that possessed more humour and personality than most people.

I've been flown around the world on great
locations working with fantastic people. We
were wild in the 1990's. We parted like rock
stars but never missed a days work. Even
through the haze of the E scene, the house wave-
where we'd be absolutely loaded all weekend I
would be back on set on Monday willing to do
anything. Drink is constantly my enemy though.
I still like a beer although it has disrupted – not
quite ruined, my career and definitely dampened
my social life and standing. I call the alcohol
demon Boozazel-

Boozazel is the demon
Revivified by drink
You're a puppet to his perversions
If you're too pissed to think

Boozazel has a mission
To corrupt and wreck your life
Turn you into a pariah
Lose your house and friends and wife.

Boozazel cannot ever die
He has a family pass
He grows in strength in youngsters
Gets stronger by the glass.

Boozazel hates a sober mind
He's shackled by the sane
Don't feed him any alcohol
-Contain his searing pain.

Boozazel's gonna take your pride
Shred all your self respect
He drives the rollercoaster ride
He's captain when you're fecked.

When work was slow over the wintertime I'd
travel to Goa, India and live like a stoner, a
blissed carefree hippy on the beach. It is there
that I met my wife Paula. The ancient gods seem
still alive there, which is laughable to such an
atheist, but there is a certain magic in the land
and the beach of Palolem always felt like a
second home – a place where I felt secure and
confident. I have three children of my own now
and I have- amazingly from such a difficult
upbringing and broken home -embraced
fatherhood and home life with a great passion.
My time with the children -Liv, Herbie and Otis-
is the most precious and enjoyable time I've
known.
I like to think I have a few defensive weapons

when my mental health deteriorates, and it does from time to time. Bouts of depression, anxiety and long hours maudlin about how I could have changed things in the past were both traits of my father and grandfather. This is an ode to my terminally reminiscing patriarchy;

It Was Better In The Past

It was better back then
In the past, now I'm old
It was lovely and sunny and sexy
Pure gold.

It was lively and funky and groovy and fast
It was better all round
Looking back at the past.

The musical scene was better than now
The age that has gone
Seemed to have the best Tao.
The fashions back then a much nicer sight
The past was all breezy and bouncy
And bright.

Now it's not nearly as fun as it used to be.
Now it's got glum. It used to be glee.

Now it's gone grey
Back then was in colour
Now all we do is worship the dollar.

These days it's hard to get anything done
Too many rules
In the past I had none
These are the days that I'm kept in check
This is the time of the 'elf/safety exec.

Back in the day I used to be keen
Back when life wasn't so sterility clean
Wishing back to the past
When I was more free
Back in the past 'for CCTV.

I had it so buzzy and now it's so bland
I acted on impulse
Not now. It's all planned
I spoke what I thought,
Not now. I'm betrayed
I'm shackled and gagged by the PC brigade.

Going out clubbing these days is a chore
Going to work is worse than before
Need to pull myself out of this place
To go back to the past-
A much nicer place.

Working hard – in the film industry- which can be at times rewarding, a stable family life, hours spent meditating playing on a bass guitar and my love of poetry writing keeps me relatively sane. I was always ridiculed by my teachers at school as I had great trouble with spelling and concentration. In fact the school-time I remember was just one big confusing rough tough waste of time taught by uninspiring and sometimes downright mean people.

It is to prove to myself - I can do it - that I am still scribbling. Though rewarding as rearranging words is it is not proving very popular with the public. I also love the creativity, love standing solo that is the art of writing, where all the wonderful characters and dialogue and plots and places are my invention alone.

Although my work in SFX has been at times very interesting and some of my colleagues usually fun to be around I've always felt to be just a tiny cog in a huge unsentimental machine that is the movie industry. We are told what to do and when and where to do it. We are the slaves to the silver screen.

The bestselling author Jasper Fforde- a lovely chap- whom I'd worked with on several productions (he was back then a focus puller) gave me a boost out of the doldrums to head for the literati when I'd learned of his publishing success. I wanted that too, to make more of a mark.

There is very little creativity in my chosen SFX field and my input in any movie that I have laboured for so many hours on has always been negligible.

With writing I am the sole creator. The artist. The director. The boss.

And So To Sawney Bean…

The Ballad of Sawney Bean
-John Nicholson, Kircudbright 1843

Go ye not by Gallowa
Come bide a while, my frein
I'll tell you o the dangers there-
Beware o Sawney Bean

There's nae body kens that he bides there
For his face is seldom seen
But tae meet his eye is tae meet your fate
At the hands of Sawney Bean

For Sawney he has taen a wife
And he's hungry bairns tae wean
And he's raised them up on the flesh o men
In the cave o Sawney Bean

And Sawney has been well endowed
Wi daughters young and lean
And they a hae taen their fathers seed
In the cave o Sawney Bean

And Sawney's sons are strong an strong
And their blades are sharp and keen
Tae spill the blood o travellers
Wha meet wi Sawney Bean

So if you ride frae there tae here
Be ye wary in between
Lest they catch your horse and spill your blood
In the cave o Sawney Bean

They'll hing ya ap an cut yer throat
An they'll pick yer carcass clean
An they'll yase yer banes ta quiet the weans
In the cave o Sawney Bean

But fear ye not, oor captain rides
On an errand o the Queen
And he carries the writ of fire and sword
For the head o Sawney Bean

They've hung them high in Edinburgh toon
And likewise aw their kin
An the wind blaws cauld on a their banes
N tae hell they a hae gaen.

When I was aged about 11 a talented young film
maker came to my house to discuss an effect
with my Father for a short film he was planning
to direct. This young man apparently had caught
the attention of the genius British director Ken
Russel and he talked about being Ken's future
understudy.

My father left the room and I asked him what his
project was about. I could not understand most
of what he said as he was so highly intellectual
and spoke in such an archaic flowery manner
that I simply sat there baffled (it turned out to be
some sort autobiographical hallucinogenic mind
fuck). He saw my confusion and then proceeded
to tell me his next, more ambitious film, The
story of Sawney Bean.

I never did get to learn his name and when I
eventually asked John who he was, my father, by
then, was far too confused to remember. He
seemed to think that the young man was killed in

a road accident a few weeks after this meeting at our house.

That terrible tale that young director told me has stayed with me since that time.

Very little information was available then about the Bean clan to a young boy from suburbia. I gathered the story first appeared in chapbooks and broadsheets collected by 'The Newgate Calendar' and published in the 1770's.

I tried writing a story about it in my early teens but could barely read my own writing, and it was crap.

And then I saw on VHS Wes Cravens' 'The Hills Have Eyes'

This fantastic cult horror film was based very loosely on the Bean legend, although set in America, and after learning this I vowed it be my premier mission to tell the original Scottish legend in all its gory glory.

For twenty years or so – on and mostly off, I have tried my hand at writing it. Partly as a creative release as the special effects department started to fracture and the more interesting parts – makeup and creature design, underwater rigging, model making etc started to have their own specialized departments leaving the likes of me operating smoke guns, operating fire and weather effects and on special occasions letting off pyrotechnics.

I have tried to write it as a novel, as movie scripts and even a theatre play. It was never quite right and all these efforts ended in the dustbin.

I realized I needed writing practice and so aged 34 set out to write (and self publish) my first complete book.

'The Damned Trip' (which I am still to this day hideously embarrassed about) is a semi autobiographical fantasy adventure about a group of film technicians who lose their minds after a magic mushroom trip and enter the faeries realm. This was kind of based on 'First Knight' a film about King Arthur, which was filmed in North Wales, when my colleague and I picked and ate too many funny fungi one lazy filming day and I ended up halfway up mount Snowdon talking to pixies that demented night. I'm relieved no one ever purchased this poor effort and it has now drifted to obscurity.

This awful book taught me one thing- that I wasn't very good at writing novels.

But I still had a story. And I needed to tell it. And so I started to try to tell it in rhyming verse..

My father in 1977 was working on Terry Gilliam's film 'Jabberwocky' where he made the complete monster.

Gilliam has always claimed he designed the Jabberwocky, taking great pride in fitting the costume backward- the 'wrong way round' onto the performance artist to solve the problem of the knees. This is not true. I remember as a seven year old boy sitting at the dining room table watching my father design the monster. I went with him to Gilliam's wacky prop filled house in London and witnessed John pitching the idea and Gilliam agreeing. I went with my father to the abattoir to collect cow and sheep stomachs, used for their interesting textures and then helped pour plaster over them for a mould. I helped pour latex rubber into the moulds to use as the Jabberwocky's skin. I helped fit the hair into the creatures head and helped sculpt and mould the horns, beak and teeth.

My father was paid a piddling amount for all this time and was never thanked or even recognised for his effort. Gilliam claimed all the glory.

 The Jabberwocky was a fixture in our living room. The great saggy breasts -removed for the film- were of special interest to me as a young boy.

I last saw it displayed in 'The London Dungeon' in the early eighties. It is probably lost to the world now.

It is still my favourite poem and I would recite it

to all my school friends. The Jabberwocky
started my interest in poetry.
I present my homage to it:

'The Jabberwocks Son'.

Twas seepig for the Jabberwocks son
The last now of his kind
For taudling through the tulgey wood
He spied the saddest find.

Yesterweek a Wizard cried
'A cure for my angina!
The flaccid should go raid the wood
To get some free vagina!'

The cull was on, the forest cleared
By vorpork sworded faeces
Who snickered here and snackered there
Wiped out majestic species.

The gentle Jubjub, for a bird
The Bander, for some snatch.
Their scalps were galumphed back to make
An aphrodisiac.

A puerk disgrace! This sterile place
Created for a habit!

For ropey munters trophy hunters
Smote all above a rabbit.

The Wizards chaste, a mental case
Whose potions fromixed harm.
Instead of mass extinction
Men should have wooed with charm.

Bereavy was the Jabberwocks boy
His bounty heart boo blooting
His fathers locks, by limpy cocks
Was boiled to get a rooting.

I believe having the towering Jabberwocky at
home was the foundation for my poetry and
hence 'Sawney's Daughter.'
I most definitely needed practice in the poetry
field and so before attempting my epic I wrote
'Judge Gruesome and his Gallant Lice' – a
bizarre little children's story poem about a brave
nit colony – 'the lice knights of the round scalp'
who try to put a stop to the evil doings of the
witch burning Judge in whose wig they live.
It is fairly good.
'Whore Town' came next, which is a
collaboration with my father. It is a rude, strange
and unpolitically correct collection of limericks,

poems and rhyming stories that I cannot ever show my children.

 It's ok, with some good poems in amongst the middling, but I needed to do that one for my father before he died. He dreamt also of becoming an author.

Both these two were a good lead up, a starting block for 'Sawney's Daughter.'

Initially I had intended to tell just the original legend as told in the first two books. My intention was to write the narrative verse in the style of 'The Rhyme of the Ancient Mariner' .

It was completed and self published on Amazon in about 2010. Fast forward a few years- with 'The Ballad Of Agnes Bean' going nowhere I decided to perform it on stage at the Edinburgh fringe festival in 2013, for some exposure.

I had an hour slot in the Surgeons Hall in the city and so had to expand the story by one more book to fill the time as each book reads to roughly 20 minutes each.

'A Ruined Hume and Bean' was thus penned.
Edinburgh was a bitter disappointment.

It was a huge expense and the children missed out on their summer holiday. It hit me hard financially with weeks taken off work (on 'Into The Woods')

It was also heart breaking in its unpopularity.

I thought Sawney Bean, being a local legend,
would put bums on seats but from a capacity of
50 I was belting out my narrative poem to 1 or 2
and sometimes not any people at all on some
dreary nights -for three full weeks.
 It was about as soul destroying as it had been
fun and fulfilling to write.
No matter. A hiccup. I couldn't stop.
I started again with the story a few years later
after I had kicked the black dog.

'The Black Dog'

If you've wrestled with the black dog
Then you know he don't fight fair
If one time you're full of beans
He'll woof you to despair.

A nasty word will call him
Or a letter in the post.
Or a posting up on Facebook
Like a dreaded inner ghost.

He's faithful if you've got him
He'll always bring you down
He'll darken up a sunny day
That damned depressing hound.

A snotty look can summon him
A glance back at the past
Jealousy will throw his stick
And he'll come running fast.

Sickness is his pack buddy
Especially of the mind
He'll root out insecurities
Present you with his find.

He'll gnaw away your happiness
As if a meaty bone
Tell you if your ghastliness
-He'll corner you alone.

I started the tale again sometime later, expanding
it to the mystery of the lost colony of Roanoke.
 Legend has it that a daughter -who birthed a
son- did escape the capture in the cave.
I have researched and included as many facts
and original names and dates from the Sawney
Bean legend and then on to the voyage and
colonization of Virginia as well as adding a few
of my own embellishments.
Who knows if James (who ruled as James 6th of
Scotland from 1567 and James 1st Of England
and Ireland after the death of Elizabeth in 1603)

did ever encounter Sawney Bean as is widely rumoured?

It is said that no official records on Sawney Bean exist but it is also true that King James was a Freemason, a deviant and a witch burning zealot who had a succession of gay lovers, most notably George Villiers, the Duke Of Buckingham, whose unpopularity led to his assassination in 1628.

James would have execute any that dared befoul his reputation so quite possibly his embarrassing meeting with the notorious cannibal has simply been erased from history to save the royal reputation.

Religious apologists have been trying to paint over these embarrassing facts for centuries to protect the 'purity' of the King James Bible. The Scottish Witchcraft Act 1563 made witchcraft and those consulting with those accused thereof a capital offence, a law which spread to England in 1604 after James's accession. He was known for personally supervising the judicial torture of women suspected of being witches. His alleged theological treatise 'Daemonologie' published in 1597 examined necromancy and black magic. 'Daemonologie' went on to become a foundation text for Shakespeare's 'Macbeth' of which

James was a patron.

Generations in Scotland's West still verify the Sawney Bean story, a story that has been passed down the ages through word of mouth.

Sawneys cave at Bennane Head can be visited as can the alleged site of the Hairy tree – the Dune tree, planted by Sawney's eldest daughter, in Girvan, in the towns Darymple street.

James 1st Did ride like a God ordained Caesar into his Romanesque coronation procession just after the plague in 1603.

Humfrey Dimmock Was a rich London Merchant who sailed with the governor John White to Roanoke and who later helped finance the disastrous rescue mission in 1589.

The authentic names and factual events on the journey aboard Raleigh's ship 'The Lion' are all documented..

The fate and history of the passenger William Brown is not recorded.

The Native American leaders Wanchese and Manteo Did visit London on two occasions in 1584 and 1585 on the invite of sir Walter Raleigh. They were both paraded at court and were an instant sensation. They went on to spend many months in the care of the scientist Thomas Harriot at Durham house where Harriot learned the Algonquin language and many an interesting fact about his guests and their Stone Age existence.

Manteo befriended Harriot and was the more affable of the two. Wanchese remained highly distrustful of the English. Wanchese thought himself more a captive than a guest during his stay. Both were said to be amazed at the wonders of modern invention and the architecture of London.

Being both 'lustie men' it is believed that they would have entertained women of negotiable affection at Durham house.

Manteo was christened on his return in 1587, the first native American to do so, and remained a friend of the English even though his mother and other members of his tribe were murdered in the mistaken revenge attack for the killing of Whites assistant George Howe.

Wanchese remained hostile.

The Meaning of CROATOAN, the word that was found carved into a tree and CRO discovered etched into a post nearby remains a mystery with many conspiracy theories surrounding it.

Edgar Allen Poe, whose most famous poem 'The Raven' (about a large talking member of the crow family and it's visit to a distraught lover and the lovers subsequent descent into madness), was found wandering in a delirium, close to death, muttering 'Croatoan!' He was found in another mans clothes and died shortly afterward.

'Croatoan' was found in the wreckage, written in the journal of aviation pioneer Amelia Earhart after her disappearance in 1937 over the Pacific.

'Croatoan' was carved into the bedpost of the last bed that he slept in of celebrated horror author and poet Ambrose Bierce before he vanished in Mexico in 1913. One of Bierce' most famous works is called 'The Death Of Halton Frayser'

It is a gothic ghost story which tells of a body skulking by night, without a soul, in a weird and horrible ensanguined wood, and a man beset by ancestral memories who met his death at the claws of that which had been his fervently loved mother.

Bierce' Mother was a descendant of William Bradford, who was a radical Puritan. Bradford escaped the persecution of James 1st when he emigrated on board 'The Mayflower.'

Black Bart (The poet), the notorious stagecoach robber, scratched 'Croatoan' into his cell wall before his release in 1888. After that day he was was never seen again.

Here is one of Black Bart's poems that he left at

the site of one of his robberies –

'Here I lay me down to sleep
To wait the coming morrow,
Perhaps success, perhaps defeat
And everlasting sorrow.
Let come what will, I'll try it on
My condition can't be worse.
And if there's munny in that box
Tis munny in my purse.'

Strangest of all it was found written in the log
book of the ghost ship ' Caroll A.Deering'
before it ran aground with no one one board, on
Cape Hatteras in 1921 – not far from what was
once called Croatoan island.
The ship was last sighted by the cape lookouts
lightship off North Carolina on January 28th
1921. The lightships keeper, captain Jacobson,
reported that a tall man with red hair had
shouted with a strange accent that the 'Deering'
had lost her anchor in a storm.
Could it be that the word 'Croatoan' had
signified the presence of the spirit of Matwau –
the fiery headed pagan God of crows?
Wahunasunocock – Pocahontas' father- Was a
powerful native war chief of at least thirty tribes
who massacred a great many people including

colonists near Chesapeake bay around 1605 partly because of predictions, warnings and omens by his priests, prophets and witch doctors.

Ananias and Eleanor, with young Virginia- the first English child born and christened in America, Did leave the fort at Roanoke alive in 1591. Ananias and Virginia's deaths are recorded, engraved on a series of rocks called 'the Dare stones' as is the birth of Eleanor's second daughter Agnes and these can be seen to this day at Brenau university, Gainesville, Georgia.

The English writer and poet William Strachey (1572-1621) whose works are among the primary sources for the colonisation of North America, wrote in his journal at Jamestown that 7 colonists, 4 men, 2 boys and a maid had escaped the Powhatan slaughter by escaping up the Chanoke river and were being held and used as copper slaves. They were protected by Chief Eyanoco at Ritanoe.

Eyanoco is said to have hated the Powhatans. William Strachey was aboard the 'Sea Venture' when it ran aground in a hurricane in Bermuda. His writings on the disaster and the state of the Jamestown colony are considered the source for Shakespeare's 'The Tempest'.

William Strachey died a pauper leaving only this verse;
'Hark! Twas the trump of death that blew
My hour has come. False world adieu
Thy pleasures have betrayed me so
That I to death untimely go

Strachey's glossary of the words of the Powhatan are one of only two records of the language.
Cannibalism Was practiced by the dread tribe Pocoughtronack as recorded by Chief Powhatan in 1607 in John Smiths journal.
French Huguenots who settled along the Tar river recorded in 1696 the Tuscarora or evil eye. These settlers saw many members of the Tuscarora tribe with grey or green eyes and red hair.
After the Tuscarora war (1711-1713) where a quarter of the Tuscarora nation were killed or enslaved and according to a Tuscarora oral tradition that lasted over a century, these descendants of the 'children of the sun god' were blamed for the misfortune. According to the legend they were being punished by their ancestors and 'The Great Spirit' for breeding with he who 'spat fire and made thunder.'
After the war anyone having the characteristics

of the Tuscarora or evil eye were blamed and isolated which accelerated the breakup of the Tuscarora nation.

Pocohontas and her husband, the tobacco entrepreneur John Rolfe, who was by then governor of the Jamestown colony, Did have an audience with King James in 1617 with Pocahontas dying of illness or poisoning after the meeting at Westminster Palace..

Later the English Did have a series of wars with the Powhatan nations, culminating in the killing of Opechancanough, Wahunsonacock's younger brother, by then himself paramount chieftain, in 1646.

Opechancanough is thought by many historians to be Don Louis- the native youth who was taken by the jesuits to Spain, Cuba and Mexico. Opechancanough later, for unexplained reasons, slaughtered the monks in their mission, where he was a guest, in Virginia thus ending Spain's ambitions to colonize the area.

Opechancanough distrusted the European settlers all his life and was responsible for the English massacres of 1622 and 1644. He was captured and killed in Jamestown in 1646 aged nearly 100.

There are still groups of Melungeons (a common Melungeon surname is Brown and Dare) in the hills of Virginia whose ancestry is a mystery but who still bare the characteristics of mixed European and indigenous genealogy.

Could it be that a Genghis Khan like figure spread far his seed four hundred years ago?

I sincerely hope dear readers that you experience just a fraction of the joy from reading it as I have from writing it.

It has been truly an epic in endeavor for me. It has been over 20 years floating around in my head and nearly 10 years writing and editing in the form that you are now reading.

Much of it was taken from extremely dark places – including a tragic fatal accident in Bulgaria on 'The Expendables 2' where a stuntman was blown up before my very eyes, a result of the pyrotechnic effect we were working on – with which through guilt ridden nightmarish dreams, enabled me to write about the horrors inside Sawney's cave in 'The Chronicle Of Thomas Hume'

To the painful penning of the voice of Matwau.

I had to travel back down a bleak and morbid memory lane to remember my mother's drunken slurry filthy ramblings in the pitch dark to give that monster his voice.

Then more joyful moments when on to the more light hearted Pythonesque innuendo and smutty dialogue.

I have enjoyed or at least been moved by the whole process.

I am constantly fighting my fierce inner critic who tells me I'm flogging a dead horse, it's crap, you can't write, no one will read it, it's niche, epic poetry is a dead art... etc

But at least now, if nothing else, I view it as mission accomplished, as an achievement.

My grandfather Frank never even started writing. He was put down so much and ridiculed by 'friends' that he was too scared to start.

I've kind of done this for him, to prove to those negative non achievers that they were wrong- as well as to prove to myself.

It may not be perfect.

The rhyme scheme shifts around and fluctuates and follows no particular pattern or rules. It is clunky in places. Some verses are far from perfect- although these are needed to link the story. It maybe considered doggerel and crude and coarse. I am not university educated. No one told me at any time I could write.

I've had to pick over every word, sentence and verse in the hundreds and hundreds of hours of editing to make it at least presentable (thank heavens for spellcheck).

I've had to rehearse and perform it out loud so as

to make sure the rhyming scheme works, for me at least, on thousands of dog walks, which has made me look a bit of a raving loony to every fellow walker.

I have often annoyed my lovely and patient wife with my manic obsession with it and the hours I spend away in a mental drift or else locked deep in edit mode.

Thanks again for purchasing, reading and if you would be so kind, reviewing my book-
'Sawney's Daughter.'

Heartfelt regards readers

Mat Horton

Please feel free to comment on 'Sawney's Daughter' by contacting me mathorton1@yahoo.co.uk or on twitter @ sawneysdaughter.